7 5⁰

THE VICAR OF WAKEFIELD

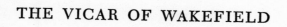

THE VICAR OF WAKEFIELD

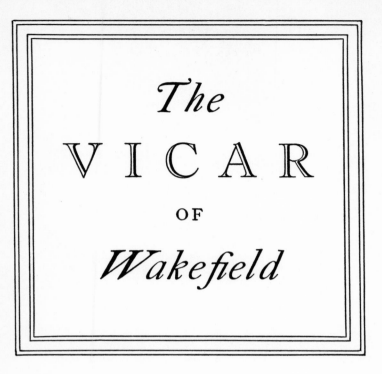

The VICAR OF *Wakefield*

BY OLIVER GOLDSMITH

ILLUSTRATED BY JOHN AUSTEN

FOR THE MEMBERS OF THE HERITAGE CLUB
NEW YORK

CONTENTS

CONTENTS

vi

CONTENTS

LIST OF COLOR PLATES

CHAPTER I

I WAS ever of opinion, that the honest man who married and brought up a large family, did more service than he who continued single and only talked of population. From this motive, I had scarce taken orders a year, before I began to think seriously of matrimony, and chose my wife, as she did her wedding-gown, not for a fine glossy surface, but such qualities as would wear well. To do her justice, she was a good-natured, notable woman; and as for breeding, there were few country ladies who could show more. She could read any English book without much spelling; but for pickling, preserving, and cookery, none could excel her. She prided herself also upon being an excellent contriver in housekeeping; though I could never find that we grew richer with all her contrivances.

However, we loved each other tenderly, and our fondness increased as we grew old. There was, in fact, nothing that could make us angry with the world or each other. We had an elegant house, situated in a fine country, and a good neighbourhood. The year was spent in a moral or rural amusement; in visiting

1

our rich neighbours, and relieving such as were poor. We had no revolutions to fear, nor fatigues to undergo; all our adventures were by the fireside, and all our migrations from the blue bed to the brown.

As we lived near the road, we often had the traveller or stranger visit us to taste our gooseberry-wine, for which we had great reputation; and I profess, with the veracity of an historian, that I never knew one of them find fault with it. Our cousins, too, even to the fortieth remove, all remembered their affinity, without any help from the herald's office, and came very frequently to see us. Some of them did us no great honour by these claims of kindred, as we had the blind, the maimed, and the halt amongst the number. However, my wife always insisted that, as they were the same *flesh and blood*, they should sit with us at the same table. So that, if we had not very rich, we generally had very happy friends about us; for this remark will hold good through life, that the poorer the guest, the better pleased he ever is with being treated; and as some men gaze with admiration at the colours of a tulip or the wing of a butterfly, so I was, by nature, an admirer of happy human faces. However, when any one of our relations was found to be a person of very bad character, a troublesome guest, or one we desired to get rid of, upon his leaving my house I ever took care to lend him a riding-coat or a pair of boots, or sometimes an horse of small value, and I always had the satisfaction of finding he never came back to return them. By this the house was cleared of such as we did not like; but never was the family of Wakefield known to turn the traveller or the poor dependant out of doors.

Thus we lived several years in a state of much happiness, not but that we sometimes had those little rubs which Providence sends to enhance the value of its favours. My orchard was often robbed by schoolboys, and my wife's custards plundered by the

2

cats or the children. The 'Squire would sometimes fall asleep in the most pathetic parts of my sermon, or his lady return my wife's civilities at church with a mutilated curtsey. But we soon got over the uneasiness caused by such accidents, and usually in three or four days began to wonder how they vexed us.

My children, the offspring of temperance, as they were educated without softness, so they were at once well formed and healthy; my sons hardy and active, my daughters beautiful and blooming. When I stood in the midst of the little circle, which promised to be the supports of my declining age, I could not avoid repeating the famous story of Count Abensberg, who, in Henry the Second's progress through Germany, while other courtiers came with their treasures, brought his thirty-two children, and presented them to his sovereign as the most valuable offering he had to bestow. In this manner, though I had but six, I considered them as a very valuable present made to my country, and consequently looked upon it as my debtor. Our eldest son was named George, after his uncle, who left us ten thousand pounds. Our second child, a girl, I intended to call after her aunt Grissel; but my wife, who during her pregnancy had been reading romances, insisted on her being called Olivia. In less than another year we had another daughter, and now I was determined that Grissel should be her name; but a rich relation taking a fancy to stand godmother, the girl was, by her directions, called Sophia; so that we had two romantic names in the family; but I solemnly protest I had no hand in it. Moses was our next, and after an interval of twelve years, we had two sons more.

It would be fruitless to deny my exultation when I saw my little ones about me; but the vanity and the satisfaction of my wife were even greater than mine. When our visitors would say, "Well, upon my word, Mrs Primrose, you have the finest children in the whole country."—"Ay, neighbour," she would answer, "they are as heaven made them—handsome enough, if they be good enough; for handsome is that handsome does." And then she would bid the girls hold up their heads, who, to conceal nothing, were certainly very handsome. Mere outside is so very trifling a circumstance with me, that I should scarce have remembered to mention it had it not been a general topic of conversation in the country. Olivia, now about eighteen, had that luxuriancy of beauty with which painters generally drew Hebe; open, sprightly, and commanding. Sophia's features were not so striking at first, but often did more certain execution; for they were soft, modest, and alluring. The one vanquished by a single blow, the other by efforts successfully repeated.

The temper of a woman is generally formed from the turn of her features; at least it was so with my daughters. Olivia wished for many lovers; Sophia to secure one. Olivia was often affected, from too great a desire to please; Sophia even repressed excellence, from her fears to offend. The one entertained me with her vivacity when I was gay; the other with her sense when I was serious. But these qualities were never carried to excess in either, and I have often seen them exchange characters for a whole day together. A suit of mourning has transformed my coquette into a prude, and a new set of ribbons has given her younger sister more than natural vivacity. My eldest son George was bred at Oxford, as I intended him for one of the learned professions. My second boy Moses, whom I designed for business, received a sort of a miscellaneous education at home. But it is needless to attempt describing the particular characters of young people that had seen but very little of the world. In short, a family likeness prevailed through all, and properly speaking, they had but one character—that of being all equally generous, credulous, simple, and inoffensive.

4

CHAPTER II

THE temporal concerns of our family were chiefly committed
to my wife's management; as to the spiritual, I took them entirely under my own direction. The profits of my living, which
amounted to but thirty-five pounds a year, I made over to the
orphans and widows of the clergy of our diocese; for, having
a fortune of my own, I was careless of temporalities, and felt a
secret pleasure in doing my duty without reward. I also set a
resolution of keeping no curate, and of being acquainted with
every man in the parish, exhorting the married men to temperance, and the bachelors to matrimony; so that in a few years it
was a common saying that there were three strange wants at
Wakefield—a parson wanting pride, young men wanting wives,
and ale-houses wanting customers.

Matrimony was always one of my favourite topics, and I
wrote several sermons to prove its happiness: but there was a
peculiar tenet which I made a point of supporting; for I maintained with Whiston, that it was unlawful for a priest of the
Church of England, after the death of his first wife, to take a

5

second; or, to express it in one word, I valued myself upon being a strict monogamist.

I was early initiated into this important dispute, on which so many laborious volumes have been written. I published some tracts upon the subject myself, which, as they never sold, I have the consolation of thinking were read only by the happy *Few*. Some of my friends called this my weak side; but, alas! they had not, like me, made it the subject of long contemplation. The more I reflected upon it, the more important it appeared. I even went a step beyond Whiston in displaying my principles; as he had engraven upon his wife's tomb that she was the *only* wife of William Whiston, so I wrote a similar epitaph for my wife, though still living, in which I extolled her prudence, economy, and obedience till death; and having got it copied fair, with an elegant frame, it was placed over the chimney-piece, where it answered several very useful purposes. It admonished my wife of her duty to me, and my fidelity to her; it inspired her with a passion for fame, and constantly put her in mind of her end.

It was thus, perhaps, from hearing marriage so often recommended, that my eldest son, just upon leaving college, fixed his affections upon the daughter of a neighbouring clergyman, who was a dignitary in the church, and in circumstances to give her a large fortune. But fortune was her smallest accomplishment. Miss Arabella Wilmot was allowed by all (except my two daughters) to be completely pretty. Her youth, health, and innocence were still heightened by a complexion so transparent, and such an happy sensibility of look, as even age could not gaze on with indifference. As Mr Wilmot knew that I could make a very handsome settlement on my son, he was not averse to the match; so both families lived together in all that harmony which generally precedes an expected alliance. Being convinced, by experience, that the days of courtship are the most happy of our lives, I was willing enough to lengthen the period; and the various amusements which the young couple every day shared in each other's company seemed to increase their passion. We were generally awaked in the morning by music, and on fine days rode a-hunting. The hours between breakfast and dinner the ladies devoted to dress and study; they usually read a page, and then gazed at themselves in the glass, which, even philosophers might own, often presented the page of greatest beauty. At dinner my wife took the lead, for, as she always insisted upon carving everything herself, it being her mother's way, she gave us upon these occasions the history of every dish. When we had dined, to prevent the ladies leaving us, I generally ordered the table to be removed; and sometimes, with the music-master's assistance, the girls would give us a very agreeable concert. Walking out, drinking tea, country dances, and forfeits shortened the rest of the day, without the assistance of cards, as I hated all manner of gaming, except back-gammon, at which my old friend and I sometimes took a twopenny hit. Nor can I here pass over an ominous circumstance that happened the last time we played together. I only wanted to fling a quatre, and yet I threw deuce ace five times running.

Some months were elapsed in this manner, till at last it was thought convenient to fix a day for the nuptials of the young couple, who seemed earnestly to desire it. During the preparations for the wedding, I need not describe the busy importance of my wife, nor the sly looks of my daughters; in fact my attention was fixed on another object—the completing a tract, which I intended shortly to publish, in defence of my favourite principle. As I looked upon this as a masterpiece, both for argument and style, I could not, in the pride of my heart, avoid showing it to my old friend Mr Wilmot, as I made no doubt of receiving his approbation: but not till too late I discovered that he was

7

most violently attached to the contrary opinion, and with good reason; for he was at that time actually courting a fourth wife. This, as may be expected, produced a dispute, attended with some acrimony, which threatened to interrupt our intended alliance; but on the day before that appointed for the ceremony, we agreed to discuss the subject at large.

It was managed with proper spirit on both sides. He asserted that I was heterodox: I retorted the charge; he replied, and I rejoined. In the meantime, while the controversy was hottest, I was called out by one of my relations, who, with a face of concern, advised me to give up the dispute, at least till my son's wedding was over. "How," cried I, "relinquish the cause of truth, and let him be a husband, already driven to the very verge of absurdity? You might as well advise me to give up my fortune as my argument."—"Your fortune," returned my friend, "I am now sorry to inform you, is almost nothing. The merchant in town, in whose hands your money was lodged, has gone off, to avoid a statute of bankruptcy, and is thought not to have left a shilling in the pound. I was unwilling to shock you or the family with the account till after the wedding; but now it may serve to moderate your warmth in the argument; for, I suppose, your own prudence will enforce the necessity of dissembling, at least till your son has the young lady's fortune secure."—"Well," returned I, "if what you tell me be true, and if I am to be a beggar, it shall never make me a rascal, or induce me to disavow my principles. I'll go this moment and inform the company of my circumstances; and as for the argument, I even here retract my former concessions in the old gentleman's favour, nor will allow him now to be an husband in any sense of the expression."

It would be endless to describe the different sensations of both families when I divulged the news of our misfortune; but what others felt was slight to what the lovers appeared to en-

8

dure. Mr Wilmot, who seemed before sufficiently inclined to break off the match, was by this blow soon determined: one virtue he had in perfection, which was prudence, too often the only one that is left us at seventy-two.

CHAPTER III

THE only hope of our family now was, that the report of our misfortune might be malicious or premature; but a letter from my agent in town soon came, with a confirmation of every particular. The loss of fortune to myself alone would have been trifling; the only uneasiness I felt was for my family, who were to be humble without an education to render them callous to contempt.

Near a fortnight had passed before I attempted to restrain their affliction; for premature consolation is but the remembrancer of sorrow. During this interval my thoughts were employed on some future means of supporting them; and at last a small Cure of fifteen pounds a year was offered me in a distant neighbourhood, where I could still enjoy my principles without molestation. With this proposal I joyfully closed, having determined to increase my salary by managing a little farm.

Having taken this resolution, my next care was to get together the wrecks of my fortune; and, all debts collected and paid, out

10

of fourteen thousand pounds we had but four hundred remaining. My chief attention, therefore, was now to bring down the pride of my family to their circumstances; for I well knew that aspiring beggary is wretchedness itself. "You cannot be ignorant, my children," cried I, "that no prudence of ours could have prevented our late misfortune; but prudence may do much in disappointing its effects. We are now poor, my fondlings, and wisdom bids us conform to our humble situation. Let us, then, without repining, give up those splendours with which numbers are wretched, and seek in humbler circumstances that peace with which all may be happy. The poor live pleasantly without our help; why, then, should not we learn to live without theirs? No, my children, let us from this moment give up all pretensions to gentility: we have still enough left for happiness if we are wise, and let us draw upon content for the deficiencies of fortune."

As my eldest son was bred a scholar, I determined to send him to town, where his abilities might contribute to our support and his own. The separation of friends and families is, perhaps, one of the most distressful circumstances attendant on penury. The day soon arrived on which we were to disperse for the first time. My son, after taking leave of his mother and the rest, who mingled their tears with their kisses, came to ask a blessing from me. This I gave him from my heart, and which, added to five guineas, was all the patrimony I had now to bestow. "You are going, my boy," cried I, "to London on foot, in the manner Hooker, your great ancestor, travelled there before you. Take from me the same horse that was given him by the good Bishop Jewel—this staff; and take this book too; it will be your comfort on the way; these two lines in it are worth a million—*I have been young, and now am old; yet never saw I the righteous man forsaken, or his seed begging their bread.* Let this be your consolation as you travel on. Go, my boy; whatever be thy fortune, let me see thee once a year; still keep a good heart, and farewell." As he was possessed of integrity and honour, I was under no apprehension from throwing him naked into the amphitheatre of life; for I knew he would act a good part, whether vanquished or victorious.

His departure only prepared the way for our own, which arrived a few days afterwards. The leaving a neighbourhood in which we had enjoyed so many hours of tranquillity was not without a tear, which scarce fortitude itself could suppress. Besides a journey of seventy miles, to a family that had hitherto never been above ten from home, filled us with apprehension; and the cries of the poor, who followed us for some miles, contributed to increase it. The first day's journey brought us in safety within thirty miles of our future retreat, and we put up for the night at an obscure inn in a village by the way. When we were shown a room, I desired the landlord, in my usual way, to let us have his company, to which he complied, as what he drank would increase the bill next morning. He knew, however, the whole neighbourhood to which I was removing, particularly 'Squire Thornhill, who was to be my landlord, and who lived within a few miles of the place. This gentleman he described as one who desired to know little more of the world than its pleasures, being particularly remarkable for his attachment for the fair sex. He observed that no virtue was able to resist his arts and assiduity, and that scarce a farmer's daughter within ten miles round but what had found him successful and faithless. Though his account gave me some pain, it had a very different effect upon my daughters, whose features seemed to brighten with the expectation of an approaching triumph; nor was my wife less pleased and confident of their allurements and virtue. While our thoughts were thus employed, the hostess entered the

12

room to inform her husband that the strange gentleman who had been two days in the house wanted money, and could not satisfy them for his reckoning. "Want money!" replied the host, "that must be impossible; for it was no later than yesterday he paid three guineas to our beadle to spare an old broken soldier that was to be whipped through the town for dog-stealing." The hostess, however, still persisting in her first assertion, he was preparing to leave the room, swearing that he would be satisfied one way or another, when I begged the landlord would introduce me to the stranger of so much charity as he described. With this he complied, showing in a gentleman who seemed to be about thirty, dressed in clothes that once were laced. His person was well formed, and his face marked with the lines of thinking. He had something short and dry in his address, and seemed not to understand ceremony, or to despise it. Upon the landlord's leaving the room, I could not avoid expressing my concern to the stranger at seeing a gentleman in such circumstances, and offered him my purse to satisfy the present demand. "I take it with all my heart, Sir," replied he, "and am glad that a late oversight in giving what money I had about me has shown me there are still some men like you. I must, however, previously entreat being informed of the name and residence of my benefactor, in order to repay him as soon as possible." In this I satisfied him fully, not only mentioning my name and late misfortunes, but the place to which I was going to remove. "This," cried he, "happens still more lucky than I hoped for, as I am going the same way myself, having been detained here two days by the floods, which I hope by to-morrow will be found passable." I testified the pleasure I should have in his company; and my wife and daughters joining in entreaty, he was prevailed upon to stay supper. The stranger's conversation, which was at once pleasing and instructive, induced me to wish for a contin-

13

uance of it; but it was now high time to retire and take refreshment against the fatigues of the following day.

The next morning we all set forward together, my family on horseback, while Mr Burchell, our new companion, walked along the footpath by the roadside, observing with a smile, that, as we were ill-mounted, he would be too generous to attempt leaving us behind. As the floods were not yet subsided, we were obliged to hire a guide, who trotted on before, Mr Burchell and I bringing up the rear. We lightened the fatigues of the road with philosophical disputes, which he seemed to understand perfectly. But what surprised me most was, that though he was a money-borrower, he defended his opinions with as much obstinacy as if he had been my patron. He now and then also informed me to whom the different seats belonged that lay in our view as we travelled the road. "That," cried he, pointing to a very magnificent house which stood at some distance, "belongs to Mr Thornhill, a young gentleman who enjoys a large fortune, though entirely dependent on the will of his uncle, Sir William Thornhill, a gentleman who, content with a little himself, permits his nephew to enjoy the rest, and chiefly resides in town." —"What!" cried I, "is my young landlord, then, the nephew of a man whose virtues, generosity, and singularities are so universally known? I have heard Sir William Thornhill represented as one of the most generous yet whimsical men in the kingdom— a man of consummate benevolence."—"Something, perhaps, too much so," replied Mr Burchell; "at least he carried benevolence to an excess when young; for his passions were then strong, and as they all were upon the side of virtue, they led it up to a romantic extreme. He early began to aim at the qualifications of the soldier and the scholar, was soon distinguished in the army, and had some reputation among men of learning. Adulation ever follows the ambitious; for such alone receive most pleasure

14

from flattery. He was surrounded with crowds, who showed him only one side of their character; so that he began to lose a regard for private interest in universal sympathy. He loved all mankind; for fortune prevented him from knowing that there were rascals. Physicians tell us of a disorder in which the whole body is so exquisitely sensible that the slightest touch gives pain. What some have thus suffered in their persons, this gentleman felt in his mind: the slightest distress, whether real or fictitious, touched him to the quick, and his soul laboured under a sickly sensibility of the miseries of others. Thus disposed to relieve, it will be easily conjectured he found numbers disposed to solicit; his profusions began to impair his fortune, but not his good-nature—that, indeed, was seen to increase as the other seemed to decay. He grew improvident as he grew poor; and though he talked like a man of sense, his actions were those of a fool. Still, however, being surrounded with importunity, and no longer able to satisfy every request that was made him, instead of *money* he gave *promises*. They were all he had to bestow, and he had not resolution enough to give any man pain by a denial. By this he drew round him crowds of dependants, whom he was sure to disappoint, yet wished to relieve. These hung upon him for a time, and left him with merited reproaches and contempt. But in proportion as he became contemptible to others, he became despicable to himself. His mind had leaned upon their adulation, and that support taken away, he could find no pleasure in the applause of his heart, which he had never learned to reverence. The world now began to wear a different aspect; the flattery of his friends began to dwindle into simple approbation; approbation soon took the more friendly form of advice; and advice, when rejected, produced their reproaches. He now, therefore, found that such friends as benefits had gathered round him were little estimable; he now found that a man's

15

own heart must be ever given to gain that of another. I now found that—that—I forgot what I was going to observe; in short, sir, he resolved to respect himself, and laid down a plan of restoring his falling fortune. For this purpose, in his own whimsical manner, he travelled through Europe on foot; and now, though he has scarce attained the age of thirty, his circumstances are more affluent than ever. At present his bounties are more rational and moderate than before; but still he preserves the character of an humorist, and finds most pleasure in eccentric virtues."

My attention was so much taken up by Mr Burchell's account that I scarce looked forward as he went along, till we were alarmed by the cries of my family; when, turning, I perceived my youngest daughter in the midst of a rapid stream, thrown from her horse, and struggling with the torrent. She had sunk twice, nor was it in my power to disengage myself in time to bring her relief. My sensations were even too violent to permit my attempting her rescue. She must have certainly perished had not my companion, perceiving her danger, instantly plunged in to her relief, and with some difficulty brought her in safety to the opposite shore. By taking the current a little further up, the rest of the family got safely over, where we had an opportunity of joining our acknowledgments to hers. Her gratitude may be more readily imagined than described; she thanked her deliverer more with looks than with words, and continued to lean upon his arm, as if still willing to receive assistance. My wife also hoped one day to have the pleasure of returning his kindness at her own house. Thus, after we were refreshed at the next inn, and had dined together, as Mr Burchell was going to a different part of the country, he took leave, and we pursued our journey, my wife observing as we went, that she liked him extremely, and protesting that if he had birth and fortune to en-

16

title him to match into such a family as ours, she knew no man she would sooner fix upon. I could not but smile to hear her talk in this lofty strain; but I was never much displeased with those harmless delusions that tend to make us more happy.

CHAPTER IV

THE place of our retreat was in a little neighbourhood consisting of farmers, who tilled their own grounds, and were equal strangers to opulence and poverty. As they had almost all the conveniences of life within themselves, they seldom visited towns or cities in search of superfluity. Remote from the polite, they still retained the primeval simplicity of manners; and, frugal by habit, they scarce knew that temperance was a virtue. They wrought with cheerfulness on days of labour, but observed festivals as intervals of idleness and pleasure. They kept up the Christmas carol, sent true love-knots on Valentine morning, ate pancakes on Shrovetide, showed their wit on the first of April, and religiously cracked nuts on Michaelmas eve. Being apprised of our approach, the whole neighbourhood came out to meet their minister, dressed in their fine clothes, and preceded by a pipe and tabor. A feast also was provided for our reception, at which we sat cheerfully down; and what the conversation wanted in wit was made up in laughter.

Our little habitation was situated at the foot of a sloping hill,

18

sheltered with a beautiful underwood behind, and a prattling river before; on the one side a meadow, on the other a green. My farm consisted of about twenty acres of excellent land, having given an hundred pound for my predecessor's good-will. Nothing could exceed the neatness of my little enclosures, the elms and hedgerows appearing with inexpressible beauty. My house consisted of but one story, and was covered with thatch, which gave it an air of snugness; the walls on the inside were nicely whitewashed, and my daughters undertook to adorn them with pictures of their own designing. Though the same room served us for parlour and kitchen, that only made it the warmer. Besides, as it was kept with the utmost neatness—the dishes, plates, and coppers being well scoured, and all disposed in bright rows on the shelves—the eye was agreeably relieved, and did not want richer furniture. There were three other apartments; one for my wife and me, another for our two daughters within our own, and the third, with two beds, for the rest of the children.

The little republic to which I gave laws was regulated in the following manner:—By sunrise we all assembled in our common apartment, the fire being previously kindled by the servant. After we had saluted each other with proper ceremony—for I always thought fit to keep up some mechanical forms of breeding, without which freedom ever destroys friendship—we all bent in gratitude to that Being who gave us another day. This duty being performed, my son and I went to pursue our usual industry abroad, while my wife and daughters employed themselves in providing breakfast, which was always ready at a certain time. I allowed half an hour for this meal, and an hour for dinner, which time was taken up in innocent mirth between my wife and daughters, and in philosophical arguments between my son and me.

As we rose with the sun, so we never pursued our labours after it was gone down, but returned home to the expecting family, where smiling looks, a neat hearth, and pleasant fire were prepared for our reception. Nor were we without guests: sometimes Farmer Flamborough, our talkative neighbour, and often the blind piper, would pay us a visit, and taste our gooseberry wine, for the making of which we had lost neither the receipt nor the reputation. These harmless people had several ways of being good company; while one played, the other would sing some soothing ballad—Johnny Armstrong's Last Goodnight, or the cruelty of Barbara Allen. The night was concluded in the manner we began the morning, my youngest boys being appointed to read the lessons of the day; and he that read loudest, distinctest, and best was to have an halfpenny on Sunday to put into the poor's box.

When Sunday came, it was indeed a day of finery, which all my sumptuary edicts could not restrain. How well soever I fancied my lectures against pride had conquered the vanity of my daughters, yet I still found them secretly attached to all their former finery; they still loved laces, ribbons, bugles, and catgut; my wife herself retained a passion for her crimson paduasoy, because I formerly happened to say it became her.

The first Sunday, in particular, their behaviour served to mortify me. I had desired my girls the preceding night to be dressed early the next day; for I always loved to be at church a good while before the rest of the congregation. They punctually obeyed my directions; but when we were to assemble in the morning at breakfast, down came my wife and daughters dressed out in all their former splendour; their hair plastered up with pomatum, their faces patched to taste, their trains bundled up into a heap behind, and rustling at every motion. I could not help smiling at their vanity, particularly that of my wife, from whom I expected more discretion. In this exigence, therefore, my only resource was to order my son, with an important air, to call our coach. The girls were amazed at the command; but I repeated it with more solemnity than before. "Surely, my dear, you jest," cried my wife; "we can walk it perfectly well; we want no coach to carry us now."—"You mistake, child," returned I, "we do want a coach; for if we walk to church in this trim, the very children in the parish will hoot after us."— "Indeed," replied my wife; "I always imagined that my Charles was fond of seeing his children neat and handsome about him." —"You may be as neat as you please," interrupted I, "and I shall love you the better for it; but all this is not neatness, but frippery. These rufflings, and pinkings and patchings will only make us hated by all the wives of our neighbours. No, my children," continued I, more gravely, "those gowns may be altered into something of a plainer cut; for finery is very unbecoming in us who want the means of decency. I do not know whether such flouncing and shredding is becoming even in the rich, if we consider, upon a moderate calculation, that the nakedness of the indigent world may be clothed from the trimmings of the vain."

This remonstration had the proper effect. They went with great composure, that very instant, to change their dress; and the next day I had the satisfaction of finding my daughters, at their own request, employed in cutting up their trains into Sunday waistcoats for Dick and Bill, the two little ones, and what was still more satisfactory, the gowns seemed improved by this curtailing.

CHAPTER V

At a small distance from the house my predecessor had made a seat overshadowed by a hedge of hawthorn and honeysuckle. Here, when the weather was fine and our labour soon finished, we usually sat together to enjoy an extensive landscape, in the calm of the evening. Here, too, we drank tea, which now was become an occasional banquet; and as we had it but seldom, it diffused a new joy, the preparations for it being made with no small share of bustle and ceremony. On these occasions our two little ones always read for us, and they were regularly served after we had done. Sometimes, to give a variety to our amusements, the girls sung to the guitar; and while they thus formed a little concert, my wife and I would stroll down the sloping field, that was embellished with blue-bells and centaury, talk of our children with rapture, and enjoy the breeze that wafted both health and harmony.

In this manner we began to find that every situation in life may bring its own peculiar pleasures: every morning waked us to a repetition of toil, but the evening repaid it with vacant hilarity.

It was about the beginning of autumn, on a holiday—for I kept such as intervals of relaxation from labour—that I had drawn out my family to our usual place of amusement, and our young musicians began their usual concert. As we were thus engaged, we saw a stag bound nimbly by, within about twenty paces of where we were sitting, and by its panting it seemed pressed by the hunters. We had not much time to reflect upon the poor animal's distress, when we perceived the dogs and horsemen come sweeping along at some distance behind, and making the very path it had taken. I was instantly for returning in with my family, but either curiosity or surprise, or some more hidden motive, held my wife and daughters to their seats. The huntsman who rode foremost passed us with great swiftness, followed by four or five persons more, who seemed in equal haste. At last a young gentleman of more genteel appearance than the rest came forward, and for a while regarding us, instead of pursuing the chase, stopped short, and giving his horse to a servant who attended, approached us with a careless, superior air. He seemed to want no introduction, but was going to salute my daughters as one certain of a kind reception; but they had early learnt the lesson of looking presumption out of countenance, upon which he let us know that his name was Thornhill, and that he was owner of the estate that lay for some extent around us. He again, therefore, offered to salute the female part of the family, and such was the power of fortune and fine clothes that he found no second repulse. As his address, though confident, was easy, we soon became more familiar; and perceiving musical instruments lying near, he begged to be favoured with a song. As I did not approve of such disproportioned acquaintances, I winked upon my daughters in order to prevent their compliance; but my hint was counteracted by one from their mother; so that, with a cheerful air, they gave us a favourite song of Dryden's. Mr Thornhill seemed highly delighted with their performance and choice, and then took up the guitar himself. He played but very indifferently; however, my eldest daughter repaid his former applause with interest, and assured him that his tones were louder than even those of her master. At this compliment he bowed, which she returned with a curtsey. He praised her taste, and she commended his understanding; an age could not have made them better acquainted; while the fond mother too, equally happy, insisted upon her landlord's stepping in and tasting a glass of her gooseberry. The whole family seemed earnest to please him: my girls attempted to entertain him with topics they thought most modern; while Moses, on the contrary, gave him a question or two from the ancients, for which he had the satisfaction of being laughed at. My little ones were no less busy, and fondly stuck close to the stranger. All my endeavours could scarce keep their dirty fingers from handling and tarnishing the lace on his clothes, and lifting up the flaps of his pocket-holes to see what was there. At the approach of evening he took leave; but not till he had requested permission to renew his visit, which, as he was our landlord, we most readily agreed to.

As soon as he was gone, my wife called a council on the conduct of the day. She was of opinion that it was a most fortunate hit; for she had known even stranger things than that brought to bear. She hoped again to see the day in which we might hold up our heads with the best of them; and concluded, she protested she could see no reason why the two Miss Wrinklers should marry great fortunes, and her children get none. As this last argument was directed to me, I protested I could see no reason for it neither; nor why Mr Simpkins got the ten thousand pound prize in the lottery, and we sat down with a blank. "I protest, Charles," cried my wife, "this is the way you always damp my girls and me when we are in spirits. Tell me, Sophy, my dear, what do you think of our new visitor? Don't you think he seemed to be good-natured?"—"Immensely so, indeed, mamma," replied she; "I think he has a great deal to say upon everything, and is never at a loss; and the more trifling the subject, the more he has to say."—"Yes," cried Olivia, "he is well enough for a man; but, for my part, I don't much like him; he is so extremely impudent and familiar; but on the guitar he is shocking." These two last speeches I interpreted by contraries. I found by this, that Sophia internally despised, as much as Olivia secretly admired him. "Whatever may be your opinions of him, my children," cried I, "to confess a truth, he has not prepossessed me in his favour. Disproportioned friendships ever terminate in disgust; and I thought, notwithstanding all his ease, that he seemed perfectly sensible of the distance between us. Let us keep to companions of our own rank. There is no character more contemptible than a man that is a fortune-hunter; and I can see no reason why fortune-hunting women should not be contemptible too. Thus, at best, we shall be contemptible if his views are honourable; but if they be otherwise!—I should shudder but to think of that. It is true, I have no apprehensions from the conduct of my children; but I think there are some from his character." I would have proceeded but for the interruption of a servant from the 'Squire, who, with his compliments, sent us a side of venison, and a promise to dine with us some days after. This well-timed present pleaded more powerfully in his favour than anything I had to say could obviate. I therefore continued silent, satisfied with just having pointed out danger, and leaving it to their own discretion to avoid it. That virtue which requires to be ever guarded is scarce worth the sentinel.

25

CHAPTER VI

As we carried on the former dispute with some degree of warmth, in order to accommodate matters, it was universally agreed that we should have a part of the venison for supper; and the girls undertook the task with alacrity. "I am sorry," cried I, "that we have no neighbour or stranger to take part in this good cheer; feasts of this kind acquire a double relish from hospitality."—"Bless me," cried my wife, "here comes our good friend Mr Burchell, that saved our Sophia, and that run you down fairly in the argument."—"Confute me in argument, child!" cried I. "You mistake there, my dear; I believe there are but few that can do that. I never dispute your abilities at making a goose-pie, and I beg you'll leave argument to me." As I spoke, poor Mr Burchell entered the house, and was welcomed by the family, who shook him heartily by the hand, while little Dick officiously reached him a chair.

I was pleased with the poor man's friendship for two reasons: because I knew that he wanted mine, and I knew him to be friendly as far as he was able. He was known in our neighbourhood by the character of the poor Gentleman, that would do no good when he was young, though he was not yet thirty. He would at intervals talk with great good sense, but in general he was fondest of the company of children, whom he used to call harmless little men. He was famous, I found, for singing them ballads and telling them stories, and seldom went out without something in his pockets for them—a piece of ginger-bread or a halfpenny whistle. He generally came for a few days into our neighbourhood once a year, and lived upon the neigh-bours' hospitality. He sat down to supper among us, and my wife was not sparing of her gooseberry wine. The tale went round; he sung us old songs, and gave the children the story of the Buck of Beverland, with the history of Patient Grissel, the adventures of Catskin, and then Fair Rosamond's Bower. Our cock, which always crew at eleven, now told us it was time for repose; but an unforeseen difficulty started about lodging the stranger—all our beds were already taken up, and it was too late to send him to the next alehouse. In this dilemma little Dick offered him his part of the bed, if his brother Moses would let him lie with him. "And I," cried Bill, "will give Mr Burchell my part, if my sisters will take me to theirs."—"Well done, my good children," cried I, "hospitality is one of the first Christian duties. The beast retires to its shelter, and the bird flies to its nest; but helpless man can only find refuge from his fellow-creature. The greatest stranger in this world was He that came to save it. He never had a house, as if willing to see what hospi-tality was left remaining among us. Deborah, my dear," cried I to my wife, "give those boys a lump of sugar each; and let Dick's be the largest, because he spoke first."

In the morning early I called out my whole family to help at saving an after-growth of hay, and our guest offering his as-sistance, he was accepted among the number. Our labours went on lightly; we turned the swath to the wind. I went foremost, and the rest followed in due succession. I could not avoid, however, observing the assiduity of Mr Burchell in assisting my daughter Sophia in her part of the task. When he had finished his own, he would join in hers, and enter into a close conversation; but I had too good an opinion of Sophia's understanding, and was too well convinced of her ambition, to be under any uneasiness from a man of broken fortune. When we were finished for the day, Mr Burchell was invited as on the night before, but he refused, as he was to lie that night at a neighbour's, to whose child he was carrying a whistle. When gone, our conversation at supper turned upon our late unfortunate guest. "What a strong instance," said I, "is that poor man of the miseries attending a youth of levity and extravagance. He by no means wants sense, which only serves to aggravate his former folly. Poor forlorn creature! where are now the revellers, the flatterers, that he could once inspire and command? Gone, perhaps, to attend the bagnio pander, grown rich by his extravagance. They once praised him, and now they applaud the pander; their former raptures at his wit are now converted into sarcasms at his folly: he is poor, and perhaps deserves poverty; for he has neither the ambition to be independent nor the skill to be useful." Prompted perhaps by some secret reasons, I delivered this observation with too much acrimony, which my Sophia gently reproved. "Whatsoever his former conduct may be, papa, his circumstances should exempt him from censure now. His present indigence is a sufficient punishment for former folly; and I have heard my papa himself say that we should never strike our unnecessary blow at a victim over whom Providence holds the scourge of its resentment."—"You are right, Sophy," cried my son Moses; "and one of the ancients finely represents so malicious a conduct by the attempts of a rustic to

28

SOPHIA AND Mr BURCHELL

flay Marsyas, whose skin, the fable tells us, had been wholly stripped off by another. Besides, I don't know if this poor man's situation be so bad as my father would represent it. We are not to judge of the feelings of others by what we might feel in their place. However dark the habitation of the mole to our eyes, yet the animal itself finds the apartment sufficiently lightsome. And, to confess a truth, this man's mind seems fitted to his station; for I never heard any one more sprightly than he was to-day, when he conversed with you." This was said without the least design; however, it excited a blush, which she strove to cover by an affected laugh, assuring him that she scarce took any notice of what he said to her, but that she believed he might once have been a very fine gentleman. The readiness with which she undertook to vindicate herself, and her blushing, were symptoms I did not internally approve; but I repressed my suspicions.

As we expected our landlord the next day, my wife went to make the venison pasty. Moses sat reading, while I taught the little ones. My daughters seemed equally busy with the rest, and I observed them for a good while cooking something over the fire. I at first supposed they were assisting their mother, but little Dick informed me in a whisper that they were making a wash for the face. Washes of all kinds I had a natural antipathy to; for I knew that, instead of mending the complexion, they spoiled it. I therefore approached my chair by sly degrees to the fire, and grasping the poker as if it wanted mending, seemingly by accident overturned the whole composition, and it was too late to begin another.

CHAPTER VII

WHEN the morning arrived on which we were to entertain our young landlord, it may be easily supposed what provisions were exhausted to make an appearance. It may also be conjectured that my wife and daughters expanded their gayest plumage on this occasion. Mr Thornhill came with a couple of friends, his chaplain and feeder. The servants, who were numerous, he politely ordered to the next ale-house, but my wife on the triumph of her heart, insisted on entertaining them all; for which, by the by, our family was pinched for three weeks after. As Mr Burchell had hinted to us the day before that he was making some proposals of marriage to Miss Wilmot, my son George's former mistress, this a good deal damped the heartiness of his reception; but accident in some measure relieved our embarrassment; for one of the company, happening to mention her name, Mr Thornhill observed, with an oath, that he never knew anything more absurd than calling such a fright a beauty: "For, strike me ugly," continued he, "if I should not find as much pleasure in choosing my mistress by the information of a lamp under the clock of St Dunstan's." At this he laughed, and so did we: the jests of the rich are ever successful. Olivia, too, could not avoid whispering, loud enough to be heard, that he had an infinite fund of humour.

After dinner I began with my usual toast, the Church. For this I was thanked by the chaplain, as he said the church was the only mistress of his affections. "Come, tell us honestly, Frank," said the 'Squire, with his usual archness, "suppose the church, your present mistress, dressed in lawn sleeves, on the one hand, and Miss Sophia with no lawn about her, on the other, which would you be for?"—"For both, to be sure," cried the chaplain. "Right, Frank," cried the 'Squire; "for may this glass suffocate me, but a fine girl is worth all the priestcraft in the creation! For what are tithes and tricks but an imposition, all a confounded imposture?—and I can prove it."—"I wish you would," cried my son Moses; "and I think," continued he, "that I should be able to answer you."—"Very well, sir," cried the 'Squire, who immediately smoked him, and winked on the rest of the company to prepare us for the sport; "if you are for a cool argument on that subject, I am ready to accept the challenge. And, first, whether are you for managing it analogically or dialogically?"—"I am for managing it rationally," cried Moses, quite happy at being permitted to dispute.—"Good again," cried the 'Squire; "and firstly, of the first. I hope you'll not deny that whatever is, is. If you don't grant me that, I can go no further."— "Why," returned Moses, "I think I may grant that, and make the best of it."—"I hope, too," returned the other, "you'll grant that a part is less than the whole."—"I grant that too," cried Moses, "it is but just and reasonable."—"I hope," cried the 'Squire, "you will not deny that the three angles of a triangle are equal to two right ones."—"Nothing can be plainer," returned t'other, and looked round with his usual importance.—"Very well," cried the

'Squire, speaking very quick, "the premisses being thus settled, I proceed to observe that the concatenation of self-existences, proceeding in a reciprocal duplicate ratio, naturally produces a problematical dialogism, which in some measure proves that the essence of spirituality may be referred to the second predicable." —"Hold, hold!" cried the other, "I deny that. Do you think that I can thus tamely submit to such heterodox doctrines?"—"What!" replied the 'Squire, as if in a passion; "not submit! Answer me one plain question: Do you think Aristotle right when he says that relatives are related?"—"Undoubtedly," replied the other. —"If so, then," cried the 'Squire, "answer me directly to what I propose: Whether do you judge the analytical investigation of the first part of my enthymem deficient secundum quoad, or quoad minus; and give me your reasons—give me your reasons, I say, directly."—"I protest," cried Moses, "I don't rightly comprehend the force of your reasoning; but if it be reduced to one simple proposition, I fancy it may then have an answer."—"Oh, sir," cried the 'Squire, "I am your most humble servant; I find you want me to furnish you with argument and intellects too. No, sir; there I protest you are too hard for me." This effectually raised the laugh against poor Moses, who sat the only dismal figure in a group of merry faces; nor did he offer a single syllable more during the whole entertainment.

But though all this gave me no pleasure, it had a very different effect upon Olivia, who mistook it for humour, though but a mere act of the memory. She thought him, therefore, a very fine gentleman; and such as consider what powerful ingredients a good figure, fine clothes, and fortune are in that character, will easily forgive her. Mr Thornhill, notwithstanding his real ignorance, talked with ease, and could expatiate upon the common topics of conversation with fluency. It is not surprising, then, that such talents should win the affections of a girl, who by education was taught to value an appearance in herself, and consequently to set a value upon it in another.

Upon his departure, we again entered into a debate upon the merits of our young landlord. As he directed his looks and conversation to Olivia, it was no longer doubted but that she was the object that induced him to be our visitor. Nor did she seem to be much displeased at the innocent raillery of her brother and sister upon this occasion. Even Deborah herself seemed to share the glory of the day, and exulted in her daughter's victory as if it were her own. "And now, my dear," cried she to me, "I'll fairly own that it was I that instructed my girls to encourage our landlord's addresses. I had always some ambition, and you see that I was right; for who knows how this may end?"—"Ay, who knows that indeed!" answered I with a groan: "for my part, I don't much like it; and I could have been better pleased with one that was poor and honest, than this fine gentleman with his fortune and infidelity; for depend on't, if he be what I suspect him, no freethinker shall ever have a child of mine."

"Sure, father," cried Moses, "you are too severe in this; for heaven will never arraign him for what he thinks, but for what he does. Every man has a thousand vicious thoughts, which arise without his power to suppress. Thinking freely of religion may be involuntary with this gentleman; so that, allowing his sentiments to be wrong, yet as he is purely passive in his assent, he is no more to be blamed for his errors than the governor of a city without walls for the shelter he is obliged to afford an invading enemy."

"True, my son," cried I; "but if the governor invites the enemy there, he is justly culpable. And such is always the case with those who embrace error. The vice does not lie in assenting to the proofs they see, but in being blind to many of the proofs that offer; so that, though our erroneous opinions be involuntary

33

when formed, yet, as we have been wilfully corrupt or very neg-
ligent in forming them, we deserve punishment for our vice or
contempt for our folly."

My wife now kept up the conversation, though not the argument. She observed that several very prudent men of our acquaintance were freethinkers, and made very good husbands;
and she knew some sensible girls that had skill enough to make
converts of their spouses. "And who knows, my dear," continued she, "what Olivia may be able to do? The girl has a great
deal to say upon every subject, and to my knowledge is very
well skilled in controversy."

"Why, my dear, what controversy can she have read?" cried
I. "It does not occur to me that I ever put such books into her
hands; you certainly overrate her merit."—"Indeed, papa," replied Olivia, "she does not; I have read a great deal of controversy. I have read the disputes between Thwackum and Square;
the controversy between Robinson Crusoe and Friday the sav-
age; and I am now employed in reading the controversy in Re-
ligious Courtship." "Very well," cried I, "that's a good girl; I
find you are perfectly qualified for making converts, and so go
help your mother to make the gooseberry pie."

CHAPTER VIII

THE next morning we were again visited by Mr Burchell,
though I began, for certain reasons, to be displeased with the
frequency of his return; but I could not refuse him my company
and fireside. It is true, his labour more than requited his entertainment; for he wrought among us with vigour, and, either in
the meadow or at the hay-rick, put himself foremost. Besides,
he had always something amusing to say that lessened our toil,
and was at once so out of the way, and yet so sensible, that I
loved, laughed at, and pitied him. My only dislike arose from
an attachment he discovered to my daughter. He would, in a
jesting manner, call her his little mistress; and when he bought
each of the girls a set of ribbons, hers was the finest. I knew not
how, but he every day seemed to become more amiable, his wit
to improve, and his simplicity to assume the superior airs of
wisdom.

Our family dined in the field, and we sat, or rather reclined,
round a temperate repast, our cloth spread upon the hay, while

35

Mr Burchell gave cheerfulness to the feast. To heighten our satisfaction, two blackbirds answered each other from opposite hedges, the familiar redbreast came and pecked the crumbs from our hands, and every sound seemed but the echo of tranquillity. "I never sit thus," says Sophia, "but I think of the two lovers, so sweetly described by Mr Gay, who were struck dead in each other's arms. There is something so pathetic in the description, that I have read it an hundred times with new rapture."—"In my opinion," cried my son, "the finest strokes in that description are much below those in the Acis and Galatea of Ovid. The Roman poet understands the use of *contrast* better; and upon that figure, artfully managed, all strength in the pathetic depends."—"It is remarkable," cried Mr Burchell, "that both the poets you mention have equally contributed to introduce a false taste into their respective countries, by loading all their lines with epithet. Men of little genius found them most easily imitated in their defects; and English poetry, like that in the latter empire of Rome, is nothing at present but a combination of luxuriant images, without plot or connection—a string of epithets that improve the sound without carrying on the sense. But perhaps, Madam, while I thus reprehend others, you'll think it just that I should give them an opportunity to retaliate; and, indeed, I have made this remark only to have an opportunity of introducing to the company a ballad, which, whatever be its other defects, is, I think, at least free from those I have mentioned."

A BALLAD

"Turn, gentle Hermit of the dale,
    And guide my lonely way
To where yon taper cheers the vale
    With hospitable ray.

THE VICAR OF WAKEFIELD

"For here forlorn and lost I tread,
  With fainting steps and slow,
Where wilds, immeasurably spread,
  Seem lengthening as I go."

"Forbear, my son," the Hermit cries,
  "To tempt the dangerous gloom;
For yonder faithless phantom flies
  To lure thee to thy doom.

"Here to the houseless child of want
  My door is open still;
And, though my portion is but scant,
  I give it with good-will.

"Then turn to-night, and freely share
  Whate'er my cell bestows;
My rushy couch and frugal fare,
  My blessing and repose.

"No flocks that range the valley free
  To slaughter I condemn;
Taught by that Power that pities me,
  I learn to pity them:

"But from the mountain's grassy side
  A guiltless feast I bring;
A scrip with herbs and fruits supplied,
  And water from the spring.

"Then, pilgrim, turn, thy cares forego;
  All earth-born cares are wrong:
Man wants but little here below,
  Nor wants that little long."

Soft as the dew from heaven descends
  His gentle accents fell:
The modest stranger lowly bends,
  And follows to the cell.

Far in a wilderness obscure
  The lonely mansion lay,
A refuge to the neighbouring poor,
  And strangers led astray.

No stores beneath its humble thatch
  Required a master's care;
The wicket, opening with a latch,
  Received the harmless pair.

And now, when busy crowds retire
  To take their evening rest,
The Hermit trimmed his little fire
  And cheered his pensive guest;

And spread his vegetable store,
  And gaily pressed and smiled,
And, skilled in legendary lore,
  The lingering hours beguiled.

Around, in sympathetic mirth,
  Its tricks the kitten tries,
The cricket chirrups on the hearth,
  The crackling faggot flies.

But nothing could a charm impart
  To soothe the stranger's woe;
For grief was heavy at his heart,
  And tears began to flow.

His rising cares the Hermit spied,
  With answering care oppressed;
And "Whence, unhappy youth," he cried,
  "The sorrows of thy breast?

"From better habitations spurned,
  Reluctant dost thou rove?
Or grieve for friendship unreturned,
  Or unregarded love?

"Alas! the joys that fortune brings
  Are trifling, and decay;
And those who prize the paltry things,
  More trifling still than they.

"And what is friendship but a name,
  A charm that lulls to sleep;
A shade that follows wealth or fame,
  But leaves the wretch to weep?

THE VICAR OF WAKEFIELD

"And love is still an emptier sound,
  The modern fair one's jest;
On earth unseen, or only found
  To warm the turtle's nest.

"For shame, fond youth, thy sorrows hush,
  And spurn the sex," he said;
But while he spoke, a rising blush
  His love-lorn guest betrayed.

Surprised, he sees new beauties rise,
  Swift mantling to the view;
Like colours o'er the morning skies,
  As bright, as transient too.

The bashful look, the rising breast,
  Alternate spread alarms;
The lovely stranger stands confessed
  A maid in all her charms.

And, "Ah! forgive a stranger rude—
  A wretch forlorn," she cried;
"Whose feet unhallowed thus intrude
  Where Heaven and you reside.

"But let a maid thy pity share,
  Whom love has taught to stray;
Who seeks for rest, but finds despair
  Companion of her way.

"My father lived beside the Tyne,
  A wealthy lord was he;
And all his wealth was marked as mine—
  He had but only me.

"To win me from his tender arms
  Unnumbered suitors came,
Who praised me for imputed charms,
  And felt, or feigned, a flame.

"Each hour a mercenary crowd
  With richest proffers strove;
Amongst the rest young Edwin bowed,
  But never talked of love.

"In humble, simple habit clad,
　　No wealth nor power had he;
Wisdom and worth were all he had,
　　But these were all to me.

"And when, beside me in the dale,
　　He carolled lays of love,
His breath lent fragrance to the gale
　　And music to the grove.

"The blossom opening to the day,
　　The dews of heaven refined,
Could nought of purity display
　　To emulate his mind.

"The dew, the blossom on the tree,
　　With charms inconstant shine:
Their charms were his, but, woe to me,
　　Their constancy was mine.

"For still I tried each fickle art,
　　Importunate and vain;
And while his passion touched my heart,
　　I triumphed in his pain:

"Till, quite dejected with my scorn,
　　He left me to my pride,
And sought a solitude forlorn,
　　In secret, where he died.

"But mine the sorrow, mine the fault,
　　And well my life shall pay;
I'll seek the solitude he sought,
　　And stretch me where he lay.

"And there, forlorn, despairing, hid,
　　I'll lay me down and die;
'Twas so for me that Edwin did,
　　And so for him will I."

"Forbid it, Heaven!" the Hermit cried,
　　And clasped her to his breast:
The wondering fair one turned to chide—
　　'Twas Edwin's self that pressed!

"Turn, Angelina, ever dear,
  My charmer, turn to see
Thine own, thy long-lost Edwin here,
  Restored to love and thee.

"Thus let me hold thee to my heart,
  And every care resign:
And shall we never, never part,
  My life,—my all that's mine?

"No, never from this hour to part,
  We'll live and love so true,
The sigh that rends thy constant heart
  Shall break thy Edwin's too."

While this ballad was reading, Sophia seemed to mix an air of tenderness with her approbation. But our tranquillity was soon disturbed by the report of a gun just by us, and immediately after a man was seen bursting through the hedge to take up the game he had killed. This sportsman was the 'Squire's chaplain, who had shot one of the blackbirds that so agreeably entertained us. So loud a report, and so near, startled my daughters; and I could perceive that Sophia, in the fright, had thrown herself into Mr Burchell's arms for protection. The gentleman came up and asked pardon for having disturbed us, affirming that he was ignorant of our being so near. He therefore sat down by my youngest daughter, and, sportsman-like, offered her what he had killed that morning. She was going to refuse, but a private look from her mother soon induced her to correct the mistake and accept his present, though with some reluctance. My wife, as usual, discovered her pride in a whisper, observing that Sophy had made a conquest of the chaplain, as well as her sister had of the 'Squire. I suspected, however, with more probability, that her affections were placed upon a different object. The chaplain's errand was to inform us that Mr Thornhill had provided music and refreshments, and intended that night giving the young ladies a ball by moonlight on the grass plot be-fore our door. "Nor can I deny," continued he, "but I have an interest in being first to deliver this message, as I expect for my reward to be honoured with Miss Sophy's hand as a partner." To this my girl replied that she should have no objection if she could do it with honour. "But here," continued she, "is a gentle-man," looking at Mr Burchell, "who has been my companion in the task for the day, and it is fit he should share in its amuse-ments." Mr Burchell returned her a compliment for her inten-tions, but resigned her up to the chaplain; adding that he was to go that night five miles, being invited to a harvest supper. His refusal appeared to me a little extraordinary; nor could I conceive how so sensible a girl as my youngest could thus pre-fer a man of broken fortunes to one whose expectations were much greater. But as men are most capable of distinguishing merit in women, so the ladies often form the truest judgments of us. The two sexes seem placed as spies upon each other, and are furnished with different abilities, adapted for mutual in-spection.

CHAPTER IX

Mr Burchell had scarce taken leave, and Sophia consented to dance with the chaplain, when my little ones came running out to tell us that the 'Squire was come with a crowd of company. Upon our return, we found our landlord with a couple of under gentlemen and two young ladies richly dressed, whom he introduced as women of very great distinction and fashion from town. We happened not to have chairs enough for the whole company; but Mr Thornhill immediately proposed, that every gentleman should sit in a lady's lap. This I positively objected to, notwithstanding a look of disapprobation from my wife. Moses was therefore dispatched to borrow a couple of chairs; and as we were in want of ladies to make up a set at country dances, the two gentlemen went with him in quest of a couple of partners. Chairs and partners were soon provided. The gentlemen returned with my neighbour Flamborough's rosy daughters, flaunting with red top-knots; but an unlucky circumtance was not adverted to—though the Miss Flamboroughs were reckoned the very best dancers in the parish, and understood the jig and the round-about to perfection, yet they were totally unacquainted with country dances. This at first discomposed us; however, after a little shoving and dragging they at last went merrily on. Our music consisted of two fiddles, with a pipe and tabor. The moon shone bright. Mr Thornhill and my eldest daughter led up the ball, to the great delight of the spectators; for the neighbours, hearing what was going forward, came flocking about us. My girl moved with so much grace and vivacity, that my wife could not avoid discovering the pride of her heart by assuring me that, though the little chit did it so cleverly, all the steps were stolen from herself. The ladies of the town strove hard to be equally easy, but without success. They swam, sprawled, languished, and frisked; but all would not do: the gazers indeed owned that it was fine; but neighbour Flamborough observed that Miss Livy's feet seemed as pat to the music as its echo. After the dance had continued about an hour, the two ladies, who were apprehensive of catching cold, moved to break up the ball. One of them, I thought, expressed her sentiments upon this occasion in a very coarse manner, when she observed, that, by the *living jingo she was all of a muck of sweat.* Upon our return to the house, we found a very elegant cold supper, which Mr Thornhill had ordered to be brought with him. The conversation at this time was more reserved than before. The two ladies threw my girls into the shade; for they would talk of nothing but high life, and high-lived company; with other fashionable topics, such as pictures, taste, Shakespeare, and the musical glasses. 'Tis true they once or twice mortified us sensibly by slipping out an oath; but that appeared to me as the surest symptom of their distinction (though I am since informed that swearing is perfectly unfashionable). Their finery, however, threw a veil over any grossness in their conversation. My daughters seemed to regard their superior accom-

44

plishments with envy; and what appeared amiss, was ascribed to tip-top quality breeding. But the condescension of the ladies was still superior to their other accomplishments. One of them observed, that had Miss Olivia seen a little more of the world, it would greatly improve her; to which the other added, that a single winter in town would make her little Sophia quite another thing. My wife warmly assented to both, adding that there was nothing she more ardently wished than to give her girls a single winter's polishing. To this I could not help replying, that their breeding was already superior to their fortune; and that greater refinement would only serve to make their poverty ridiculous, and give them a taste for pleasures they had no right to possess. "And what pleasures," cried Mr Thornhill, "do they not deserve to possess, who have so much in their power to bestow? As for my part," continued he, "my fortune is pretty large; love, liberty, and pleasure are my maxims; but curse me, if a settlement of half my estate could give my charming Olivia pleasure, it should be hers; and the only favour I would ask in return would be to add myself to the benefit." I was not such a stranger to the world as to be ignorant that this was the fashionable cant to disguise the insolence of the basest proposal; but I made an effort to suppress my resentment. "Sir," cried I, "the family which you now condescend to favour with your company has been bred with as nice a sense of honour as you. Any attempts to injure that may be attended with very dangerous consequences. Honour, sir, is our only possession at present, and of that last treasure we must be particularly careful." I was soon sorry for the warmth with which I had spoken this, when the young gentleman, grasping my hand, swore he commended my spirit, though he disapproved my suspicions. "As to your present hint," continued he, "I protest that nothing was farther from my heart than such a thought. No, by all that's tempting! the virtue that will stand a regular siege was never to my taste; for all my amours are carried by a coup-de-main."

The two ladies, who affected to be ignorant of the rest, seemed highly displeased with this last stroke of freedom, and began a very discreet and serious dialogue upon virtue; in this, my wife, the chaplain, and I soon joined; and the 'Squire himself was at last brought to confess a sense of sorrow for his former excesses. We talked of the pleasures of temperance, and of the sunshine in the mind unpolluted with guilt. I was so well pleased, that my little ones were kept up beyond the usual time to be edified by so much good conversation. Mr Thornhill even went beyond me, and demanded if I had any objection to giving prayers. I joyfully embraced the proposal; and in this manner the night was passed in the most comfortable way, till at last the company began to think of returning. The ladies seemed very unwilling to part with my daughters, for whom they had conceived a particular affection, and joined in a request to have the pleasure of their company home. The 'Squire seconded the proposals, and my wife added her entreaties; the girls, too, looked upon me as if they wished to go. In this perplexity, I made two or three excuses, which my daughters as readily removed: so that at last I was obliged to give a peremptory refusal, for which we had nothing but sullen looks and short answers the whole day ensuing.

CHAPTER X

I now began to find that all my long and painful lectures upon temperance, simplicity, and contentment were entirely disregarded. The distinctions lately paid us by our betters awaked that pride which I had laid asleep, but not removed. Our windows, again, as formerly, were filled with washes for the neck and face. The sun was dreaded as an enemy to the skin without doors, and the fire as a spoiler of the complexion within. My wife observed that rising too early would hurt her daughters' eyes, that working after dinner would redden their noses; and she convinced me that the hands never looked so white as when they did nothing. Instead therefore of finishing George's shirts, we now had them new-modelling their old gauzes, or flourishing upon catgut. The poor Miss Flamboroughs, their former gay companions, were cast off as mean acquaintance, and the whole conversation ran upon high life, and high-lived company, with pictures, taste, Shakespeare, and the musical glasses.

But we could have borne all this, had not a fortune-telling gipsy come to raise us into perfect sublimity. The tawny sibyl

47

no sooner appeared, than my girls came running to me for a shilling a-piece to cross her hand with silver. To say the truth, I was tired of being always wise, and could not help gratifying their request, because I loved to see them happy. I gave each of them a shilling; though for the honour of the family it must be observed, that they never went without money themselves, as my wife always generously let them have a guinea each, to keep in their pockets, but with strict injunctions never to change it. After they had been closeted up with the fortune-teller for some time, I knew by their looks, upon their returning, that they had been promised something great. "Well, my girls, how have you sped? Tell me, Livy, has the fortune-teller given thee a penny-worth?"—"I protest, papa," says the girl, "I believe she deals with somebody that's not right; for she positively declared, that I am to be married to a 'Squire in less than a twelvemonth!"—"Well, now, Sophy, my child," said I, "and what sort of an husband are you to have?"—"Sir," replied she, "I am to have a Lord soon after my sister has married the 'Squire."—"How!" cried I, "is that all you are to have for your two shillings? Only a Lord and a 'Squire for two shillings? You fools, I could have promised you a Prince and a Nabob for half the money."

This curiosity of theirs, however, was attended with very serious effects: we now began to think ourselves designed by the stars to do something exalted, and already anticipated our future grandeur.

It has been a thousand times observed, and I must observe it once more, that the hours we pass with happy prospects in view, are more pleasing than those crowned with fruition. In the first case, we cook the dish to our own appetite; in the latter Nature cooks it for us. It is impossible to repeat the train of agreeable reveries we called up for our entertainment. We looked upon our fortunes as once more rising; and, as the whole parish asserted that the 'Squire was in love with my daughter, she was actually so with him; for they persuaded her into the passion. In this agreeable interval my wife had the most lucky dreams in the world, which she took care to tell us every morning, with great solemnity and exactness. It was one night a coffin and cross-bones, the signs of an approaching wedding; at another time she imagined her daughters' pockets filled with farthings, a certain sign they would shortly be stuffed with gold. The girls themselves had their omens. They felt strange kisses on their lips; they saw rings in the candle; purses bounced from the fire, and true-love-knots lurked in the bottom of every teacup.

Towards the end of the week we received a card from the town ladies, in which, with their compliments, they hoped to see all our family at church the Sunday following. All Saturday morning I could perceive, in consequence of this, my wife and daughters in close conference together, and now and then glancing at me with looks that betrayed a latent plot. To be sincere, I had strong suspicions that some absurd proposal was preparing for appearing with splendour the next day. In the evening they began their operations in a very regular manner, and my wife undertook to conduct the siege. After tea, when I seemed in spirits, she began thus:—"I fancy, Charles, my dear, we shall have a great deal of good company at our church to-morrow." —"Perhaps we may, my dear," returned I, "though you need be under no uneasiness about that; you shall have a sermon whether there be or not."—"That is what I expect," returned she; "but I think, my dear, we ought to appear there as decently as possible, for who knows what may happen?"—"Your precautions," replied I, "are highly commendable. A decent behaviour and appearance in church is what charms me. We should be devout and humble, cheerful and serene."—"Yes," cried she, "I know that; but I mean we should go there in as proper a manner as possible; not altogether like the scrubs about us."—"You are quite right, my dear," returned I, "and I was going to make the very same proposal. The proper manner of going is to go there as early as possible, to have time for meditation before the service begins."—"Phoo, Charles," interrupted she, "all that is very true; but not what I would be at; I mean, we should go there genteelly. You know the church is two miles off, and I protest I don't like to see my daughters trudging up to their pew all blowzed and red with walking, and looking for all the world as if they had been winners at a smock race. Now, my dear, my proposal is this: there are our two plough-horses, the colt that has been in our family these nine years, and his companion Blackberry, that has scarce done an earthly thing for this month past. They are both grown fat and lazy. Why should not they do something as well as we? And let me tell you, when Moses has trimmed them a little, they will cut a very tolerable figure."

To this proposal I objected that walking would be twenty times more genteel than such a paltry conveyance, as Blackberry was wall-eyed, and the colt wanted a tail; that they had never been broke to the rein, but had a hundred vicious tricks; and that we had but one saddle and pillion in the whole house. All these objections, however, were overruled; so that I was obliged to comply. The next morning I perceived them not a little busy in collecting such materials as might be necessary for the expedition; but, as I found it would be a business of time, I walked on to the church before, and they promised speedily to follow. I waited near an hour in the reading desk for their arrival; but not finding them come as expected, I was obliged to begin, and went through the service, not without some uneasiness at finding them absent. This was increased, when all was finished, and no appearance of the family. I therefore walked back by the horse-way, which was five miles round, though the footway was

THE HERITAGE
Sandglass

The classics which are our heritage from the past in Editions which will be the heritage of the future

NUMBER 3C

ISSUED MONTHLY TO THE MEMBERS
OF THE HERITAGE CLUB
595 MADISON AVENUE, NEW YORK

"When Lovely Woman Stoops to Folly"

IT was only last month that we sent you our eager members a new edition of Goethe's masterpiece, *Faust,* and begged you to prize it highly. Now, since Goethe is in your minds and hearts, we ask you to wonder what Goethe himself prized highly, for we are in position to tell you. Goethe, the great Goethe, was nuts about *The Vicar of Wakefield*. He said it was the greatest novel of the eighteenth century; repeatedly he acknowledged his own debt to it.

Even when Oliver Goldsmith was alive, it would have been said that this was a crying shame, that the author of *The Vicar of Wakefield* knew nothing of the fame which was to come to his masterpiece. He did not know that Goethe, the great Goethe, would call it the greatest novel of his day. He did not know that Charles Dickens would take a copy of *The Vicar of Wakefield* to bed with him, night after night.

He was born in 1728, in Ireland, the son of an Irish clergyman. Although *The Vicar of Wakefield* was first published in 1766, it was probably written in 1762. For it was in October 1762 that Oliver Goldsmith sold a one-third share of *The Vicar of Wakefield* to a man named Benjamin Collins. This man Collins printed the first edition of *The Vicar of Wakefield* in 1766. Eight years later, he disposed of his share in the work for the astonishing sum of five guineas: so you can easily conclude how much Collins must have paid for his share twelve years earlier!

Goldsmith had been, like his father before him, "generous and credulous and simple". When he was twenty-five, he went to Edinburgh to study medicine; but he quickly got tired of medicine and went wandering through Europe, on foot, playing a flute. He studied medicine again in Padua, and went back to England to practice. But he failed in the practice of medicine, and became a writer.

When he died, in 1774, he left two thousand pounds in debts. But he had written *The Deserted Village,* he had written *She Stoops to Conquer,* he had written *The Vicar of Wakefield.*

The Vicar of Wakefield caught on as soon as Goldsmith died. It has appeared in hundreds of editions, it has been translated into a dozen languages. Of all those pieces of fine literature which depend for their charm on the presentment of the simpler life and emotion amid the sweet country scenes around old England's homes, no book has taken so strong a hold upon the affection of all conditions of men the world over, as has Oliver Goldsmith's *The Vicar of Wakefield.* Walter Scott said "we read it in youth and age; we return to it again and again, and bless the memory of an author who contrives so well to reconcile us to human nature."

The charm of this novel lies in the fact that it is written with an art which is perfect artlessness. It is written with a perfect style, through which flows a stream of pure feeling and fine humanity. The perfec-

tion of its style is evidenced by the fact that any reader, be he barber or billionaire, be she maiden or manicurist, feels an instant sympathy with all of the characters. The Vicar himself, the unruly Sophia, the dependable Mr. Burchell, the reprehensible Squire Thornhill, the simple Moses, all become parts of our lives as we read of them. We chuckle when they chuckle, we weep when they weep. The book is full of gentle satire, and our emotions are stirred by the satire. But the book is a biography of a man of a true gentleness and pure feeling, of as fine a humanity, as ever lived.

Goethe found inspiration in this book. Dickens took it to bed to read every night. Samuel Johnson read it over and over, for he said that Oliver Goldsmith "wrote like an angel". Now you our eager members will be in position to read *The Vicar of Wakefield* in a fine edition, for now we the directors of The Heritage Club send you a copy of *The Vicar of Wakefield* in what we consider a truly fine edition.

The inspiration for the edition springs from John Austen. Mr. Austen is an Englishman, who lives quietly with his wife in a town near Canterbury, in a house which looks like the Castle of Otranto, on a farm which is called Hearts Delight. For Mr. Austen the farm *is* heart's delight, although it takes its name from the prosaic fact that it was once the delight of a farmer named Hart. In this sweet English country atmosphere, John Austen has steeped himself in the England of the last half of the eighteenth century. During his earlier years, he illustrated books as though he were a new Beardsley. Now that he lives in the heart of the English countryside, he is preoccupied with the England of a bygone day, and his pen makes pictures full of the charm of that England.

John Austen has illustrated nearly fifty books, and is possibly the best known, in America, of all the English illustrators. His greatest success in America came when he illustrated *Vanity Fair* for The Limited Editions Club. And now he has illustrated *The Vicar of Wakefield* in the style in which he illustrated *Vanity Fair*.

He has made a series of portraits, in color, of all the principal characters. These portraits are done in line and in colors of extreme delicacy. In their portraits, the Vicar and Mr. Burchell, Sophia and Squire Thornhill, all come alive in a vale of tears. Mr. Austen brings them alive with a slightly archaic touch, so that they posture like characters upon Greek vases; but Mr. Austen loves them, he loves their costumes, he loves their mannered gestures, and he draws them with tears running down his cheeks. These portraits therefore give an atmosphere to the book, or else we miss our guess, an atmosphere both wistful and tender.

Mr. Austen has also done a series of thirty-one line drawings, each drawing appearing at the head of one of the chapters. The line of his drawings is pure, almost Grecian in its purity, and the illustrations again are wistful and tender, if they are anything.

We turned the Austen illustrations over to John Fass, and we told John Fass that we hoped he would design a volume for our members in which the wistful and tender atmosphere is tenderly preserved. We leave it to you, to determine whether Mr. Fass has done so.

He has designed a book of which the page is 6¼ x 9½ inches in size, and in which there are 256 pages.

The type specified by Mr. Fass is an utterly new type, a type called Caledonia. The letters of this type were drawn by that great American artist-of-the-book, the sage of Hingham Center, William Addison Dwiggins. He drew these letters for the Mergenthaler Linotype Company.

When he began to draw this type, he wanted to modify the type which is called Scotch Roman. That type has been used previously in our books, and is used in the setting of *The Sketch Book of Geoffrey Crayon,* which you will see next month. It is a sound and workable type, which has served the printing craft for a hundred years. But Bill Dwiggins decided that there are a few features about it which are not quite happy. The fact that he has christened his new type Caledonia shows that he has kept its Scotch ancestry in his mind. But he has created a type which is more slender in the drawing of the letters, more lively as one looks at a page of it, than the Scotch; yet has much of the quality of robustness, of simplicity, of hardworkingness, which Scotch has.

It is probable that you will see more of the Caledonia type. It is being used in the setting of our forthcoming edition of *Gulliver's Travels;* and it will be used time upon time again, for it is a safe prediction that Caledonia will become one of the famous types in which to set books.

In setting *The Vicar of Wakefield,* Caledonia is used in the twelve-point size, on fifteen-point linotype slugs, which means that there are three points of leading between the lines. If all of this sounds feverishly technical to you, you must only remember that the result gives you a brave and readable page, a page which caresses your eye and makes you want to read it.

The pages set in Caledonia type are printed on a smooth, white and distinguished paper made for this book by the Curtis Paper Company. Then the pages are gathered and folded and bound into boards. Over the boards is worked a coarse and attractive linen, dyed an unusual rose color.

This rose color seems to us to have a tender and archaic charm about it. The stamping of the title on the cover, and the slip-case selected to hold the book, are both intended to preserve this quality. *The Vicar of Wakefield* is a book of tender charm; and John Austen's illustrations, and John Fass' typographic plans, the paper and the rose colored binding are all intended to preserve this tender charm. If the intention is realized, if you are made more aware of the charm of *The Vicar of Wakefield* when reading it in this edition, then the arts of the book will in this case not have been used in vain.

but two, and, but when got about half-way home, perceived the procession marching slowly forward towards the church; my son, my wife, and the two little ones exalted on one horse, and my two daughters upon the other. I demanded the cause of their delay; but I soon found by their looks they had met with a thousand misfortunes on the road. The horses had at first refused to move from the door, till Mr Burchell was kind enough to beat them forward for about two hundred yards with his cudgel. Next, the straps of my wife's pillion broke down, and they were obliged to stop to repair them before they could proceed. After that, one of the horses took it into its head to stand still, and neither blows nor entreaties could prevail with him to proceed. It was just recovering from this dismal situation that I found them; but perceiving everything safe, I own their present mortification did not much displease me, as it would give me many opportunities of future triumph, and teach my daughters more humility.

CHAPTER XI

MICHAELMAS-EVE happening on the next day, we were invited to burn nuts and play tricks at neighbour Flamborough's. Our late mortifications had humbled us a little, or it is probable we might have rejected such an invitation with contempt; however, we suffered ourselves to be happy. Our honest neighbour's goose and dumplings were fine, and the lamb's-wool, even in the opinion of my wife, who was a connoisseur, was excellent. It is true, his manner of telling stories was not quite so well. They were very long, and very dull, and all about himself, and we had laughed at them ten times before: however, we were kind enough to laugh at them once more.

Mr Burchell, who was of the party, was always fond of seeing some innocent amusement going forward, and set the boys and girls to blind-man's buff. My wife, too, was persuaded to join in the diversion, and it gave me pleasure to think she was not yet too old. In the meantime, my neighbour and I looked on, laughed at every feat, and praised our own dexterity when we were young. Hot cockles succeeded next, questions and commands followed that, and last of all, they sat down to hunt the slipper. As every person may not be acquainted with this primeval pastime, it may be necessary to observe, that the company at this play plant themselves in a ring upon the ground, all except one, who stands in the middle, whose business it is to catch a shoe, which the company shove about under their hams from one to another, something like a weaver's shuttle. As it is impossible, in this case, for the lady who is up to face all the company at once, the great beauty of the play lies in hitting her a thump with the heel of the shoe on that side least capable of making a defence. It was in this manner that my eldest daughter was hemmed in, and thumped about, all blowzed, in spirits, and bawling for fair play, fair play, with a voice that might deafen a ballad-singer, when, confusion on confusion! who should enter the room but our two great acquaintances from town, Lady Blarney and Miss Carolina Wilelmina Amelia Skeggs! Description would but beggar, therefore it is unnecessary to describe, this new mortification. Death! To be seen by ladies of such high breeding in such vulgar attitudes! Nothing better could ensue from such a vulgar play of Mr Flamborough's proposing. We seemed struck to the ground for some time, as if actually petrified with amazement.

The two ladies had been at our house to see us, and finding us from home, came after us hither, as they were uneasy to know what accident could have kept us from church the day before. Olivia undertook to be our prolocutor, and delivered the whole in a summary way, only saying, "We were thrown from our horses." At which account the ladies were greatly concerned; but being told the family received no hurt, they were extremely glad; but being informed that we were almost killed by the fright, they were vastly sorry; but hearing that we had a very good night, they were extremely glad again. Nothing could exceed their complaisance to my daughters: their professions the last evening were warm, but now they were ardent. They protested a desire of having a more lasting acquaintance. Lady Blarney was particularly attached to Olivia; Miss Carolina Wilelmina Amelia Skeggs (I love to give the whole name) took a greater fancy to her sister. They supported the conversation between themselves, while my daughters sat silent, admiring their exalted breeding. But as every reader, however beggarly himself, is fond of high-lived dialogues, with anecdotes of Lords, Ladies, and Knights of the Garter, I must beg leave to give him the concluding part of the present conversation.

"All that I know of the matter," cried Miss Skeggs, "is this, that it may be true or may not be true; but this I can assure your Ladyship, that the whole rout was in amaze; his Lordship turned all manner of colours, my Lady fell into a swound, but Sir Tomkyn drawing his sword, swore he was hers to the last drop of his blood."

"Well," replied our Peeress, "this I can say, that the Duchess never told me a syllable of the matter, and I believe her Grace would keep nothing a secret from me. This you may depend upon as fact, that the next morning my Lord Duke cried out three times to his valet-de-chambre, Jernigan! Jernigan! Jernigan! bring me my garters."

But previously I should have mentioned the very impolite behaviour of Mr Burchell, who, during this discourse, sat with his face turned to the fire, and, at the conclusion of every sentence, would cry out *fudge*, an expression which displeased us all, and in some measure damped the rising spirit of the conversation.

"Besides, my dear Skeggs," continued our Peeress, "there is nothing of this in the copy of verses that Dr Burdock made upon the occasion."—*Fudge!*

"I am surprised at that," cried Miss Skeggs: "for he seldom

54

leaves anything out, as he writes only for his own amusement. But can your Ladyship favour me with a sight of them?"—*Fudge!*

"My dear creature," replied our Peeress, "do you think I carry such things about me? Though they are very fine, to be sure, and I think myself something of a judge—at least I know what pleases myself. Indeed, I was ever an admirer of all Dr Burdock's little pieces; for except what he does, and our dear Countess at Hanover Square, there's nothing comes out but the most lowest stuff in nature; not a bit of high life among them."—*Fudge!*

"Your Ladyship should except," says the other, "your own things in the Lady's Magazine. I hope you'll say there's nothing low-lived there? But I suppose we are to have no more from that quarter?"—*Fudge!*

"Why, my dear," says the lady, "you know my reader and companion has left me, to be married to Captain Roach, and as my poor eyes won't suffer me to write myself, I have been for some time looking out for another. A proper person is no easy matter to find; and, to be sure, thirty pounds a year is a small stipend for a well-bred girl of character, that can read, write, and behave in company; as for the chits about town, there is no bearing them about one."—*Fudge!*

"That I know," cried Miss Skeggs, "by experience. For of the three companions I had this last half year, one of them refused to do plain-work an hour in the day; another thought twenty-five guineas a year too small a salary; and I was obliged to send away the third, because I suspected an intrigue with the chaplain. Virtue, my dear Lady Blarney, virtue is worth any price; but where is that to be found?"—*Fudge!*

My wife had been, for a long time, all attention to this discourse, but was particularly struck with the latter part of it.

55

Thirty pounds and twenty-five guineas a year, made fifty-six pounds five shillings English money, all which was in a manner going a-begging, and might easily be secured in the family. She for a moment studied my looks for approbation; and, to own a truth, I was of opinion, that two such places would fit our two daughters exactly. Besides, if the 'Squire had any real affection for my eldest daughter, this would be the way to make her every way qualified for her fortune. My wife, therefore, was resolved that we should not be deprived of such advantages for want of assurance, and undertook to harangue for the family. "I hope," cried she, "your Ladyships will pardon my present presumption. It is true, we have no right to pretend to such favours; but yet it is natural for me to wish putting my children forward in the world. And, I will be bold to say, my two girls have had a pretty good education and capacity; at least the country can't show better. They can read, write, and cast accounts; they understand their needle, broad-stitch, cross and change, and all manner of plainwork; they can pink, point, and frill, and know something of music; they can do up small clothes, work upon catgut; my eldest can cut paper, and my youngest has a very pretty manner of telling fortunes upon the cards."—*Fudge!*

When she had delivered this pretty piece of eloquence, the two ladies looked at each other a few minutes in silence, with an air of doubt and importance. At last Miss Carolina Wilelmina Amelia Skeggs condescended to observe that the young ladies, from the opinion she could form of them from so slight an acquaintance, seemed very fit for such employments. "But a thing of this kind, madam," cried she, addressing my spouse, "requires a thorough examination into characters, and a more perfect knowledge of each other. Not, Madam," continued she, "that I in the least suspect the young ladies' virtue, prudence, and dis-

56

cretion: but there is a form in these things, Madam—there is a form."

My wife approved her suspicions very much, observing that she was very apt to be suspicious herself, but referred her to all the neighbours for a character; but this our Peeress declined as unnecessary, alleging that her cousin Thornhill's recommendation would be sufficient; and upon this we rested our petition.

CHAPTER XII

WHEN we were returned home, the night was dedicated to schemes of future conquest. Deborah exerted much sagacity in conjecturing which of the two girls was likely to have the best place, and most opportunities of seeing good company. The only obstacle to our preferment was in obtaining the 'Squire's recommendation; but he had already shown us too many instances of his friendship to doubt of it now. Even in bed my wife kept up the usual theme: "Well, faith, my dear Charles, between ourselves I think we have made an excellent day's work of it."—"Pretty well!" cried I, not knowing what to say. "What, only pretty well!" returned she: "I think it is very well. Suppose the girls should come to make acquaintances of taste in town! This I am assured of, that London is the only place in the world for all manner of husbands. Besides, my dear, stranger things happen every day; and as ladies of quality are so taken with my daughters, what will not men of quality be? *Entre nous*, I protest I like my Lady Blarney vastly—so very obliging. However, Miss Carolina Wilelmina Amelia Skeggs has my warm heart.

58

But yet, when they came to talk of places in town, you saw at once how I nailed them. Tell me, my dear, don't you think I did for my children there?"—"Ay," returned I, not knowing well what to think of the matter; "Heaven grant they may be both the better for it this day three months!" This was one of those observations I usually made to impress my wife with an opinion of my sagacity: for if the girls succeeded, then it was a pious wish fulfilled; but if anything unfortunate ensued, then it might be looked upon as a prophecy. All this conversation, however, was only preparatory to another scheme; and indeed I dreaded as much. This was nothing less than that, as we were now to hold up our heads a little higher in the world, it would be proper to sell the Colt, which was grown old, at a neighbouring fair, and buy us a horse that would carry a single or double upon an occasion, and make a pretty appearance at church, or upon a visit. This at first I opposed stoutly; but it was stoutly defended. However, as I weakened, my antagonist gained strength, till at last it was resolved to part with him.

As the fair happened on the following day, I had intentions of going myself; but my wife persuaded me that I had got a cold, and nothing could prevail upon her to permit me from home. "No, my dear," said she, "our son Moses is a discreet boy, and can buy and sell to a very good advantage; you know all our great bargains are of his purchasing. He always stands out and higgles, and actually tires them till he gets a bargain."

As I had some opinion of my son's prudence, I was willing enough to entrust him with this commission; and the next morning I perceived his sisters mighty busy in fitting out Moses for the fair: trimming his hair, brushing his buckles, and cocking his hat with pins. The business of the toilet being over, we had at last the satisfaction of seeing him mounted upon the Colt, with a deal box before him to bring home groceries in. He had on a coat made of that cloth they call thunder-and-lightning, which, though grown too short, was much too good to be thrown away. His waistcoat was of gosling green, and his sisters had tied his hair with a broad black ribbon. We all followed him several paces from the door bawling after him, "Good luck! good luck!" till we could see him no longer.

He was scarce gone, when Mr Thornhill's butler came to congratulate us upon our good fortune, saying that he overheard his young master mention our names with great commendation.

Good fortune seemed not to come alone. Another footman from the same family followed, with a card for my daughters, importing that the two ladies had received such pleasing accounts from Mr Thornhill of us all, that after a few previous inquiries they hoped to be perfectly satisfied. "Ay," cried my wife, "I now see it is no easy matter to get into the families of the great; but when one once gets in, then, as Moses says, one may go to sleep." To this piece of humour, for she intended it for wit, my daughters assented with a loud laugh of pleasure. In short, such was her satisfaction at this message, that she actually put her hand in her pocket and gave the messenger sevenpence halfpenny.

This was to be our visiting day. The next that came was Mr Burchell, who had been at the fair. He brought my little ones a pennyworth of gingerbread each, which my wife undertook to keep for them, and gave them by letters at a time. He brought my daughters also a couple of boxes, in which they might keep wafers, snuff, patches, or even money, when they got it. My wife was usually fond of a weasel-skin purse, as being the most lucky; but this by the by. We had still a regard for Mr Burchell, though his late rude behaviour was in some measure displeasing; nor could we now avoid communicating our happiness to him, and asking his advice: although we seldom followed advice, we were

60

MOSES PREPARES FOR MARKET

all ready enough to ask it. When he read the note from the two ladies, he shook his head, and observed, that an affair of this sort demanded the utmost circumspection. This air of diffidence highly displeased my wife. "I never doubted, sir," cried she, "your readiness to be against my daughters and me. You have more circumspection than is wanted. However, I fancy when we come to ask advice, we will apply to persons who seem to have made use of it themselves."—"Whatever my own conduct may have been, Madam," replied he, "is not the present question: though, as I have made no use of advice myself, I should in conscience give it to those that will." As I was apprehensive this answer might draw on a repartee, making up by abuse what it wanted in wit, I changed the subject, by seeming to wonder what could keep our son so long at the fair, as it was now almost nightfall. "Never mind our son," cried my wife; "depend upon it he knows what he is about. I'll warrant we'll never see him sell his hen on a rainy day. I have seen him buy such bargains as would amaze one. I'll tell you a good story about that, that will make you split your sides with laughing.—But, as I live, yonder comes Moses, without a horse, and the box at his back."

As she spoke, Moses came slowly on foot, and sweating under the deal box, which he had strapt round his shoulders like a pedlar. "Welcome, welcome, Moses! well, my boy, what have you brought us from the fair?"—"I have brought you myself," cried Moses, with a sly look, and resting the box on the dresser. "Ay, Moses," cried my wife, "that we know; but where is the horse?" —"I have sold him," cried Moses, "for three pounds five shillings and twopence."—"Well done, my good boy," returned she; "I knew you would touch them off. Between ourselves, three pounds five shillings and twopence is no bad day's work. Come, let us have it then."—"I have brought back no money," cried Moses again. "I have laid it all out in a bargain, and here it is," pulling out a bundle from his breast: "here they are; a gross of green spectacles, with silver rims and shagreen cases."—"A gross of green spectacles!" repeated my wife in a faint voice. "And you have parted with the Colt, and brought us back nothing but a gross of green paltry spectacles!"—"Dear mother," cried the boy, "why won't you listen to reason? I had them a dead bargain, or I should not have bought them. The silver rims alone will sell for double the money."—"A fig for the silver rims," cried my wife, in a passion: "I dare swear they won't sell for above half the money at the rate of broken silver, five shillings an ounce."—"You need be under no uneasiness," cried I, "about selling the rims, for they are not worth sixpence; for I perceive they are only copper varnished over."—"What!" cried my wife, "not silver! the rims not silver!"—"No," cried I, "no more silver than your saucepan."—"And so," returned she, "we have parted with the Colt, and have only got a gross of green spectacles, with copper rims and shagreen cases? A murrain take such trumpery! The blockhead has been imposed upon, and should have known his company better."—"There, my dear," cried I, "you are wrong; he should not have known them at all."—"Marry, hang the idiot!" returned she, "to bring me such stuff: if I had them, I would throw them in the fire."—"There again you are wrong, my dear," cried I; "for though they be copper, we will keep them by us, as copper spectacles, you know, are better than nothing."

By this time the unfortunate Moses was undeceived. He now saw that he had indeed been imposed upon by a prowling sharper, who, observing his figure, had marked him for an easy prey. I therefore asked the circumstances of his deception. He sold the horse, it seems, and walked the fair in search of another. A reverend-looking man brought him to a tent, under the pretence of having one to sell. "Here," continued Moses, "we met another man, very well dressed, who desired to borrow twenty pounds upon these, saying that he wanted money, and would dispose of them for a third of the value. The first gentleman, who pretended to be my friend, whispered me to buy them, and cautioned me not to let so good an offer pass. I sent for Mr Flamborough, and they talked him up as finely as they did me; and so at last we were persuaded to buy the two gross between us."

CHAPTER XIII

Our family had now made several attempts to be fine; but some unforeseen disaster demolished each as soon as projected. I endeavoured to take the advantage of every disappointment to improve their good sense, in proportion as they were frustrated in ambition. "You see, my children," cried I, "how little is to be got by attempts to impose upon the world in coping with our betters. Such as are poor, and will associate with none but the rich, are hated by those they avoid, and despised by those they follow. Unequal combinations are always disadvantageous to the weaker side, the rich having the pleasure, and the poor the inconveniences that result from them. But come, Dick, my boy, and repeat the fable you were reading to-day, for the good of the company."

"Once upon a time," cried the child, "a Giant and a Dwarf were friends, and kept together. They made a bargain that they would never forsake each other, but go seek adventures. The first battle they fought was with two Saracens, and the Dwarf, who was very courageous, dealt one of the champions a most angry blow. It did the Saracen but very little injury, who, lifting up his sword, fairly struck off the poor Dwarf's arm. He was now in a woful plight; but the Giant, coming to his assistance, in a short time left the two Saracens dead on the plain, and the Dwarf cut off the dead man's head out of spite. They then travelled on to another adventure. This was against three bloody-minded Satyrs, who were carrying away a damsel in distress. The Dwarf was not quite so fierce now as before, but for all that struck the first blow, which was returned by another that knocked out his eye; but the Giant was soon up with him, and had they not fled, would certainly have killed them every one. They were all very joyful for this victory, and the damsel, who was relieved, fell in love with the Giant, and married him. They now travelled far, and farther than I can tell, till they met with a company of robbers. The Giant, for the first time, was foremost now; but the Dwarf was not far behind. The battle was stout and long. Wherever the Giant came, all fell before him; but the Dwarf had liked to have been killed more than once. At last the victory declared for the two adventurers; but the Dwarf lost his leg. The Dwarf had now lost an arm, a leg, and an eye, while the Giant was without a single wound; upon which he cried out to his little companion, 'My little hero, this is glorious sport! let us get one victory more, and then we shall have honour for ever.'—'No,' cries the Dwarf, who was by this time grown wiser, 'no, I declare off; I'll fight no more; for I find in every battle that you get all the honour and rewards, but all the blows fall upon me.' "

I was going to moralise this fable, when our attention was called off to a warm dispute between my wife and Mr Burchell upon my daughters' intended expedition to town. My wife very strenuously insisted upon the advantages that would result from it; Mr Burchell, on the contrary, dissuaded her with great ardour; and I stood neuter. His present dissuasions seemed but the second part of those which were received with so ill a grace in the morning. The dispute grew high; while poor Deborah, instead of reasoning stronger, talked louder, and at last was obliged to take shelter from a defeat in clamour. The conclusion of her harangue, however, was highly displeasing to us all. She knew, she said, of some who had their own secret reasons for what they advised; but, for her part, she wished such to stay away from her house for the future. "Madam," cried Burchell, with looks of great composure, which tended to inflame her the more, "as for secret reasons, you are right: I have secret reasons, which I forbear to mention, because you are not able to answer those of which I make no secret; but I find my visits here are become troublesome; I'll take my leave, therefore, now, and perhaps come once more to take a final farewell when I am quitting the country." Thus saying, he took up his hat; nor could the attempts of Sophia, whose looks seemed to upbraid his precipitancy, prevent his going.

When gone, we all regarded each other for some minutes with confusion. My wife, who knew herself to be the cause, strove to hide her concern with a forced smile and an air of assurance, which I was willing to reprove. "How, woman," cried I to her, "is it thus we treat strangers? Is it thus we return their kindness? Be assured, my dear, that these were the harshest words, and to me the most unpleasing, that ever escaped your lips!"— "Why would he provoke me, then?" replied she; "but I know the motives of his advice perfectly well. He would prevent my girls from going to town that he may have the pleasure of my youngest daughter's company here at home. But, whatever happens, she shall choose better company than such low-lived fellows as he."—"Low-lived, my dear, do you call him?" cried I; "it is very possible we may mistake this man's character, for he seems, upon some occasions, the most finished gentleman I ever knew. Tell me, Sophia, my girl, has he ever given you any secret instances of his attachment?"—"His conversation with me, Sir," replied my daughter, "has ever been sensible, modest, and pleasing. As to ought else—no, never. Once, indeed, I remember to have heard him say, he never knew a woman who could find merit in a man that seemed poor."—"Such, my dear," cried I, "is the common cant of all the unfortunate or idle. But I hope you have been taught to judge properly of such men, and that it would be even madness to expect happiness from one who has been so very bad an economist of his own. Your mother and I have now better prospects for you. The next winter, which you will probably spend in town, will give you opportunities of making a more prudent choice."

What Sophia's reflections were upon this occasion I cannot pretend to determine; but I was not displeased at the bottom that we were rid of a guest from whom I had much to fear. Our breach of hospitality went to my conscience a little; but I quickly silenced that monitor by two or three specious reasons, which served to satisfy and reconcile me to myself. The pain which conscience gives the man who has already done wrong is soon got over. Conscience is a coward; and those faults it has not strength enough to prevent, it seldom has justice enough to accuse.

CHAPTER XIV

THE journey of my daughters to town was now resolved upon, Mr Thornhill having kindly promised to inspect their conduct himself, and inform us by letter of their behaviour. But it was thought indispensably necessary that their appearance should equal the greatness of their expectations, which could not be done without expense. We debated therefore in full council what were the easiest methods of raising money, or, more properly speaking, what we could most conveniently sell. The deliberation was soon finished: it was found that our remaining horse was utterly useless for the plough without his companion, and equally unfit for the road, as wanting an eye: it was therefore determined that we should dispose of him, for the purposes above mentioned, at the neighbouring fair; and to prevent imposition, that I should go with him myself. Though this was one of the first mercantile transactions of my life, yet I had no doubt about acquitting myself with reputation. The opinion a man forms of his own prudence is measured by that of the company he keeps: and as mine was most in the family way, I had conceived no unfavourable sentiments of my worldly wisdom. My wife, however, next morning, at parting, after I had got some paces from the door, called me back to advise me, in a whisper, to have all my eyes about me.

I had, in the usual forms, when I came to the fair, put my horse through all his paces, but for some time had no bidders. At last a chapman approached, and after he had for a good while examined the horse round, finding him blind of one eye, he would have nothing to say to him; a second came up, but observing that he had a spavin, declared he would not take him for the driving home; a third perceived he had a wind-gall, and would bid no money; a fourth knew by his eye that he had the botts; a fifth wondered what a plague I could do at the fair with a blind, spavined, galled hack, that was only fit to be cut up for a dog kennel. By this time, I began to have a most hearty contempt for the poor animal myself, and was almost ashamed at the approach of every customer; for though I did not entirely believe all the fellows told me, yet I reflected that the number of witnesses was a strong presumption they were right; and St Gregory, upon Good Works, professes himself to be of the same opinion.

I was in this mortifying situation, when a brother clergyman, an old acquaintance, who had also business at the fair, came up, and, shaking me by the hand, proposed adjourning to a public-house, and taking a glass of whatever we could get. I readily closed with the offer, and entering an alehouse, we were shown into a little back room, where was only a venerable old man, who sat wholly intent over a large book, which he was reading. I never in my life saw a figure that prepossessed me more favourably. His locks of silver grey venerably shaded his temples, and his green old age seemed to be the result of health and benevolence. However, his presence did not interrupt our conversation: my friend and I discoursed on the various turns of fortune we had met; the Whistonian controversy, my last pamphlet, the archdeacon's reply, and the hard measure that was dealt me. But our attention was in a short time taken off, by the appearance of a youth, who, entering the room, respectfully said something softly to the old stranger. "Make no apologies, my child," said the old man; "to do good is a duty we owe to all our fellow-creatures. Take this, I wish it were more; but five pounds will relieve your distress, and you are welcome." The modest youth shed tears of gratitude, and yet his gratitude was scarce equal to mine. I could have hugged the good old man in my arms, his benevolence pleased me so. He continued to read, and we resumed our conversation, until my companion, after some time, recollecting that he had business to transact in the fair, promised to be soon back; adding, that he always desired to have as much of Dr Primrose's company as possible. The old gentleman, hearing my name mentioned, seemed to look at me with attention for some time; and when my friend was gone, most respectfully demanded if I was any way related to the great Primrose, that courageous monogamist, who had been the bulwark of the Church. Never did my heart feel sincerer rapture than at that moment. "Sir," cried I, "the applause of so good a man as I am sure you are, adds to that happiness in my breast which your benevolence has already excited. You behold before you, Sir, that Dr Primrose, the monogamist, whom you have been pleased to call great. You here see that unfortunate divine, who has so long, and it would ill become me to say, successfully fought against the deuterogamy of the age."—"Sir," cried the stranger, struck with awe, "I fear I have been too familiar, but you'll forgive my curiosity, Sir: I beg pardon."—"Sir," cried I, grasping his hand, "you are so far from displeasing me by your familiarity, that I must beg you'll accept my friendship,

70

as you have already my esteem."—"Then with gratitude I accept the offer," cried he, squeezing me by the hand, "thou glorious pillar of unshaken orthodoxy! and do I behold"——I here interrupted what he was going to say; for though, as an author, I could digest no small share of flattery, yet now my modesty would permit no more. However, no lovers in romance ever cemented a more instantaneous friendship. We talked upon several subjects: at first I thought he seemed rather devout than learned, and began to think he despised all human doctrines as dross. Yet this no way lessened him in my esteem, for I had for some time begun privately to harbour such an opinion myself. I therefore took occasion to observe, that the world in general began to be blameably indifferent as to doctrinal matters, and followed human speculations too much. "Ay, Sir," replied he, as if he had reserved all his learning to that moment, "Ay, Sir, the world is in its dotage; and yet the cosmogony, or creation of the world, has puzzled philosophers of all ages. What a medley of opinions have they not broached upon the creation of the world! Sanchoniathon, Manetho, Berosus, and Ocellus Lucanus, have all attempted it in vain. The latter has these words, *Anarchon ara kai atelutaion to pan,* which imply that all things have neither beginning nor end. Manetho also, who lived about the time of Nebuchadon-Asser—Asser being a Syriac word, usually applied as a surname to the kings of that country, as Teglat Phael-Asser, Nabon-Asser—he, I say, formed a conjecture equally absurd; for as we usually say, *ek to biblion kubernetes,* which implies that books will never teach the world; so he attempted to investigate—— But, Sir, I ask pardon, I am straying from the question." —That he actually was; nor could I, for my life, see how the creation of the world had anything to do with the business I was talking of; but it was sufficient to show me that he was a man of letters, and I now reverenced him the more. I was resolved, therefore, to bring him to the touchstone; but he was too mild and too gentle to contend for victory. Whenever I made an observation that looked like a challenge to controversy, he would smile, shake his head, and say nothing; by which I understood he could say much, if he thought proper. The subject, therefore, insensibly changed from the business of antiquity, to that which brought us both to the fair: mine, I told him, was to sell a horse, and very luckily, indeed, his was to buy one for one of his tenants. My horse was soon produced; and, in fine, we struck a bargain. Nothing now remained but to pay me, and he accordingly pulled out a thirty pound note, and bid me change it. Not being in a capacity of complying with this demand, he ordered his footman to be called up, who made his appearance in a very genteel livery. "Here, Abraham," cried he, "go and get gold for this; you'll do it at neighbour Jackson's or anywhere." While the fellow was gone, he entertained me with a pathetic harangue on the great scarcity of silver, which I undertook to improve, by deploring also the great scarcity of gold; so that, by the time Abraham returned, we had both agreed that money was never so hard to be come at as now. Abraham returned to inform us, that he had been over the whole fair, and could not get change, though he had offered half-a-crown for doing it. This was a very great disappointment to us all; but the old gentleman, having paused a little, asked me if I knew one Solomon Flamborough in my part of the country. Upon replying that he was my next-door neighbour: "If that be the case, then," returned he, "I believe we shall deal. You shall have a draft upon him, payable at sight; and, let me tell you, he is as warm a man as any within five miles round him. Honest Solomon and I have been acquainted for many years together. I remember I always beat him at three jumps; but he could hop on one leg further than I." A draft upon my neighbour was to me the same as money; for I was sufficiently convinced of his ability. The draft was signed, and put into my hands, and Mr Jenkinson, the old gentleman, his man Abraham, and my horse, old Blackberry, trotted off very well pleased with each other.

After a short interval, being left to reflection, I began to recollect that I had done wrong in taking a draft from a stranger, and so prudently resolved upon following the purchaser, and having back my horse. But this was now too late; I therefore made directly homewards, resolving to get the draft changed into money at my friend's as fast as possible. I found my honest neighbour smoking his pipe at his own door, and informing him that I had a small bill upon him, he read it twice over. "You can read the name, I suppose," cried I—"Ephraim Jenkinson."— "Yes," returned he, "the name is written plain enough, and I know the gentleman too—the greatest rascal under the canopy of heaven. This is the very same rogue who sold us the spectacles. Was he not a venerable-looking man, with grey hair, and no flaps to his pocket-holes? And did he not talk a long string of learning about Greek, and cosmogony, and the world?" To this I replied with a groan. "Ay," continued he, "he has but that one piece of learning in the world, and he always talks it away whenever he finds a scholar in company; but I know the rogue, and will catch him yet."

Though I was already sufficiently mortified, my greatest struggle was to come, in facing my wife and daughters. No truant was ever more afraid of returning to school, there to behold the master's visage, than I was of going home. I was determined, however, to anticipate their fury, by first falling into a passion myself.

But, alas! upon entering, I found the family no way disposed for battle. My wife and girls were all in tears, Mr Thornhill having been there that day to inform them that their journey to town was entirely over. The two ladies, having heard reports of us from some malicious person about us, were that day set out for London. He could neither discover the tendency nor the author of these; but whatever they might be, or whoever might have broached them, he continued to assure our family of his friendship and protection. I found, therefore, that they bore my disappointment with great resignation, as it was eclipsed in the greatness of their own. But what perplexed us most, was to think who could be so base as to asperse the character of a family so harmless as ours; too humble to excite envy, and too inoffensive to create disgust.

CHAPTER XV

THAT evening, and a part of the following day, was employed in fruitless attempts to discover our enemies: scarcely a family in the neighbourhood but incurred our suspicions, and each of us had reasons for our opinions best known to ourselves. As we were in this perplexity, one of our little boys, who had been playing abroad, brought in a letter-case, which he found on the green. It was quickly known to belong to Mr Burchell, with whom it had been seen, and, upon examination, contained some hints upon different subjects; but what particularly engaged our attention was a sealed note, superscribed, *the copy of a letter to be sent to the ladies at Thornhill Castle.* It instantly occurred that he was the base informer, and we deliberated whether the note should not be broken open. I was against it; but Sophia, who said she was sure that of all men he would be the last to be guilty of so much baseness, insisted upon its being read. In this she was seconded by the rest of the family, and at their joint solicitation I read as follows:—

"Ladies,—The bearer will sufficiently satisfy you as to the person from whom this comes: one at least the friend of innocence, and ready to prevent its being seduced. I am informed for a truth, that you have some intention of bringing two young ladies to town, whom I have some knowledge of, under the character of companions. As I would neither have simplicity imposed upon, nor virtue contaminated, I must offer it as my opinion, that the impropriety of such a step will be attended with dangerous consequences. It has never been my way to treat the infamous or the lewd with severity; nor should I now have taken this method of explaining myself, or reproving folly, did it not aim at guilt. Take, therefore, the admonition of a friend, and seriously reflect on the consequences of introducing infamy and vice into retreats where peace and innocence have hitherto resided."

Our doubts were now at an end. There seemed, indeed, something applicable to both sides in this letter, and its censures might as well be referred to those to whom it was written, as to us; but the malicious meaning was obvious, and we went no farther. My wife had scarcely patience to hear me to the end, but railed at the writer with unrestrained resentment. Olivia was equally severe, and Sophia seemed perfectly amazed at his baseness. As for my part, it appeared to me one of the vilest instances of unprovoked ingratitude I had met with; nor could I account for it in any other manner than by imputing it to his desire of detaining my youngest daughter in the country, to have the more frequent opportunities of an interview. In this manner we all sat ruminating upon schemes of vengeance, when our other little boy came running in to tell us that Mr Burchell was approaching at the other end of the field. It is easier to conceive than describe the complicated sensations which are felt from the pain of a recent injury, and the pleasure of approaching vengeance. Though our intentions were only to upbraid him with

76

his ingratitude, yet it was resolved to do it in a manner that would be perfectly cutting. For this purpose we agreed to meet him with our usual smiles; to chat in the beginning with more than ordinary kindness, to amuse him a little; and then, in the midst of the flattering calm, to burst upon him like an earthquake, and overwhelm him with a sense of his own baseness. This being resolved upon, my wife undertook to manage the business herself, as she really had some talents for such an undertaking. We saw him approach; he entered, drew a chair, and sat down. "A fine day, Mr Burchell."—"A very fine day, Doctor; though I fancy we shall have some rain by the shooting of my corns."—"The shooting of your horns!" cried my wife, in a loud fit of laughter, and then asked pardon for being fond of a joke. "Dear madam," replied he, "I pardon you with all my heart, for I protest I should not have thought it a joke had you not told me."—"Perhaps not, Sir," cried my wife, winking at us; "and yet I dare say you can tell us how many jokes go to an ounce."—"I fancy, madam," returned Burchell, "you have been reading a jest book this morning, that ounce of jokes is so very good a conceit; and yet, madam, I had rather see half an ounce of understanding."—"I believe you might," cried my wife, still smiling at us, though the laugh was against her; "and yet I have seen some men pretend to understanding that have very little." —"And no doubt," returned her antagonist, "you have known ladies set up for wit that had none." I quickly began to find that my wife was likely to gain but little at this business; so I resolved to treat him in a style of more severity myself. "Both wit and understanding," cried I, "are trifles, without integrity; it is that which gives value to every character. The ignorant peasant without fault is greater than the philosopher with many; for what is genius or courage without an heart?

"'An honest man's the noblest work of God.'"

"I always held that hackneyed maxim of Pope," returned Mr Burchell, "as very unworthy a man of genius, and a base desertion of his own superiority. As the reputation of books is raised, not by their freedom from defect, but the greatness of their beauties; so should that of men be prized, not for their exemption from fault but the size of those virtues they are possessed of. The scholar may want prudence, the statesman may have pride, and the champion ferocity; but shall we prefer to these the low mechanic, who laboriously plods on through life without censure or applause? We might as well prefer the tame correct paintings of the Flemish school to the erroneous but sublime animations of the Roman pencil."

"Sir," replied I, "your present observation is just, when there are shining virtues and minute defects; but when it appears that great vices are opposed in the same mind to as extraordinary virtues, such a character deserves contempt."

"Perhaps," cried he, "there may be some such monsters as you describe, of great vices joined to great virtues; yet in my progress through life, I never yet found one instance of their existence: on the contrary, I have ever perceived, that where the mind was capacious, the affections were good. And indeed Providence seems kindly our friend in this particular, thus to debilitate the understanding where the heart is corrupt, and diminish the power where there is the will to do mischief. This rule seems to extend even to other animals: the little vermin race are ever treacherous, cruel, and cowardly, whilst those endowed with strength and power are generous, brave, and gentle."

"These observations sound well," returned I, "and yet it would be easy this moment to point out a man," and I fixed my eye steadfastly upon him, "whose head and heart form a most detestable contrast. Ay, Sir," continued I, raising my voice, "and I am glad to have this opportunity of detecting him in the midst

78

of his fancied security. Do you know this, Sir, this pocket-book?"
—"Yes, Sir," returned he, with a face of impenetrable assurance,
"that pocket-book is mine, and I am glad you have found it."—
"And do you know," cried I, "this letter? Nay, never falter, man,
but look me full in the face; I say do you know this letter?"—
"That letter?" returned he; "yes, it was I that wrote that letter."—
"And how could you," said I, "so basely, so ungratefully presume
to write this letter?"—"And how came you," replied he, with
looks of unparalleled effrontery, "so basely to presume to break
open this letter? Don't you know, now, I could hang you all for
this? All that I have to do is to swear at the next justice's that
you have been guilty of breaking open the lock of my pocket-
book, and so hang you all up at his door." This piece of unexpected insolence raised me to such a pitch, that I could scarce
govern my passion. "Ungrateful wretch! begone, and no longer
pollute my dwelling with thy baseness! begone, and never let
me see thee again! Go from my door, and the only punishment
I wish thee is an alarmed conscience, which will be a sufficient
tormentor!" So saying, I threw him his pocket-book, which he
took up with a smile, and shutting the clasps with the utmost
composure, left us, quite astonished at the serenity of his assurance. My wife was particularly enraged that nothing could make
him angry, or make him seem ashamed of his villainies: "My
dear," cried I, willing to calm those passions that had been raised
too high among us, "we are not to be surprised that bad men
want shame: they only blush at being detected in doing good,
but glory in their vices.

"Guilt and Shame, says the allegory, were at first companions,
and, in the beginning of their journey, inseparably kept together. But their union was soon found to be disagreeable and
inconvenient to both. Guilt gave Shame frequent uneasiness,
and Shame often betrayed the secret conspiracies of Guilt. After

79

long disagreement, therefore, they at length consented to part for ever. Guilt boldly walked forward alone, to overtake Fate, that went before in the shape of an executioner; but Shame, being naturally timorous, returned back to keep company with Virtue, which in the beginning of their journey they had left behind. Thus, my children, after men have travelled through a few stages in vice, shame forsakes them, and returns back to wait upon the few virtues they have still remaining."

CHAPTER XVI

Whatever might have been Sophia's sensations, the rest of the family was easily consoled for Mr Burchell's absence by the company of our landlord, whose visits now became more frequent, and longer. Though he had been disappointed in procuring my daughters the amusements of the town, as he designed, he took every opportunity of supplying them with those little recreations which our retirement would admit of. He usually came in the morning; and, while my son and I followed our occupations abroad, he sat with the family at home, and amused them by describing the town, with every part of which he was particularly acquainted. He could repeat all the observations that were retailed in the atmosphere of the play-houses, and had all the good things of the high wits by rote, long before they made their way into the jest books. The intervals between conversation were employed in teaching piquet, or sometimes in setting my two little ones to box, to make them *sharp*, as he called it: but the hopes of having him for a son-in-law in some measure blinded us to all his imperfections. It must be owned, that my wife laid a thousand schemes to entrap him; or to speak it more tenderly, used every art to magnify the merit of her daughter. If the cakes at tea ate short and crisp, they were made by Olivia; if the gooseberry wine was well knit, the gooseberries were of her gathering: it was her fingers which gave the pickles their peculiar green; and, in the composition of a pudding, it was her judgment that mixed the ingredients. Then the poor woman would sometimes tell the 'Squire, that she thought him and Olivia extremely of a size, and would bid both stand up to see which was the tallest. These instances of cunning, which she thought impenetrable, yet which everybody saw through, were very pleasing to our benefactor, who gave every day some new proofs of his passion, which, though they had not arisen to proposals of marriage, yet we thought fell but little short of it; and his slowness was attributed sometimes to native bashfulness, and sometimes to his fear of offending his uncle. An occurrence, however, which happened soon after, put it beyond a doubt that he designed to become one of our family; my wife even regarded it as an absolute promise.

My wife and daughters happening to return a visit to neighbour Flamborough's, found that family had lately got their pictures drawn by a limner, who travelled the country, and took likeness for fifteen shillings a head. As this family and ours had long a sort of rivalry in point of taste, our spirit took the alarm at this stolen march upon us; and, notwithstanding all I could say, and I said much, it was resolved that we should have our pictures done too.

Having, therefore, engaged the limner,—for what could I do? —our next deliberation was to show the superiority of our tastes in the attitudes. As for our neighbour's family, there were seven of them, and they were drawn with seven oranges,—a thing quite out of taste, no variety in life, no composition in the world.

We desired to have something in a brighter style; and, after many debates, at length came to a unanimous resolution of being drawn together, in one large historical family piece. This would be cheaper, since one frame would serve for all, and it would be infinitely more genteel; for all families of any taste were now drawn in the same manner. As we did not immediately recollect an historical subject to hit us, we were contented each with being drawn as independent historical figures. My wife desired to be represented as Venus, and the painter was desired not to be too frugal of his diamonds in her stomacher and hair. Her two little ones were to be as Cupids by her side; while I, in my gown and band, was to present her with my books on the Whistonian controversy. Olivia would be drawn as an Amazon, sitting upon a bank of flowers, dressed in a green joseph, richly laced in gold, and a whip in her hand. Sophia was to be a shepherdess, with as many sheep as the painter could put in for nothing; and Moses was to be dressed out with a hat and white feather. Our taste so much pleased the 'Squire, that he insisted on being put in as one of the family, in the character of Alexander the Great, at Olivia's feet. This was considered by us all as an indication of his desire to be introduced into the family, nor could we refuse his request. The painter was therefore set to work, and, as he wrought with assiduity and expedition, in less than four days the whole was completed. The piece was large, and, it must be owned, he did not spare his colours; for which my wife gave him great encomiums. We were all perfectly satisfied with his performance; but an unfortunate circumstance had not occurred till the picture was finished, which now struck us with dismay. It was so very large, that we had no place in the house to fix it. How we all came to disregard so material a point is inconceivable; but certain it is, we had been all greatly remiss. The picture, therefore, instead of gratifying our vanity, as we hoped, leaned, in a most mortifying manner, against the kitchen wall, where the canvas was stretched and painted, much too large to be got through any of the doors, and the jest of all our neighbours. One compared it to Robinson Crusoe's long-boat, too large to be removed; another thought it more resembled a reel in a bottle; some wondered how it could be got out, but still more were amazed how it ever got in.

But though it excited the ridicule of some, it effectually raised more malicious suggestions in many. The 'Squire's portrait being found united with ours was an honour too great to escape envy. Scandalous whispers began to circulate at our expense, and our tranquillity was continually disturbed by persons, who came as friends to tell us what was said of us by enemies. These reports we always resented with becoming spirit; but scandal ever improves by opposition.

We once again, therefore, entered into a consultation upon obviating the malice of our enemies, and at last came to a resolution which had too much cunning to give me entire satisfaction. It was this: as our principal object was to discover the honour of Mr Thornhill's addresses, my wife undertook to sound him, by pretending to ask his advice in the choice of a husband for her eldest daughter. If this was not found sufficient to induce him to a declaration, it was then resolved to terrify him with a rival. To this last step, however, I would by no means give my consent, till Olivia gave me the most solemn assurances that she would marry the person provided to rival him upon this occasion, if he did not prevent it by taking her himself. Such was the scheme laid, which, though I did not strenuously oppose, I did not entirely approve.

The next time, therefore, that Mr Thornhill came to see us, my girls took care to be out of the way, in order to give their mamma an opportunity of putting her scheme in execution; but they only retired to the next room, from whence they could overhear the whole conversation. My wife artfully introduced it, by observing that one of the Miss Flamboroughs was like to have a very good match of it in Mr Spanker. To this the 'Squire assenting, she proceeded to remark, that they who had warm fortunes were always sure of getting good husbands: "But Heaven help," continued she, "the girls that have none! What signifies beauty, Mr Thornhill? or what signifies all the virtue, and all the qualifications in the world, in this age of self-interest? It is not, What is she? but, What has she? is all the cry."

"Madam," returned he, "I highly approve the justice, as well as the novelty, of your remarks; and if I were a king, it should be otherwise. It should then, indeed, be fine times with the girls without fortunes: our two young ladies should be the first for whom I would provide."

"Ah, Sir," returned my wife, "you are pleased to be facetious: but I wish I were a queen, and then I know where my eldest daughter should look for a husband. But, now that you have put it into my head, seriously, Mr Thornhill, can't you recommend me a proper husband for her! She is now nineteen years old, well grown, and well educated, and, in my humble opinion, does not want for parts."

"Madam," replied he, "if I were to choose, I would find out a person possessed of every accomplishment that can make an angel happy. One with prudence, fortune, taste, and sincerity; such, madam, would be, in my opinion, the proper husband."— "Ay, Sir," said she, "but do you know of any such person?"— "No, madam," returned he, "it is impossible to know any person that deserves to be her husband: she's too great a treasure for one man's possession; she's a goddess! Upon my soul, I speak what I think—she's an angel!"—"Ah, Mr Thornhill, you only flatter my poor girl: but we have been thinking of marrying her

85

to one of your tenants, whose mother is lately dead, and who wants a manager; you know whom I mean,—farmer Williams; a warm man, Mr Thornhill, able to give her good bread, and who has several times made her proposals" (which was actually the case); "but, Sir," concluded she, "I should be glad to have your approbation of our choice." "How, madam," replied he, "my approbation!—my approbation of such a choice! Never. What! sacrifice so much beauty, and sense, and goodness, to a creature insensible of the blessing! Excuse me, I can never approve of such a piece of injustice. And I have my reasons."— "Indeed, Sir," cried Deborah, "if you have your reasons, that's another affair; but I should be glad to know those reasons."— "Excuse me, madam," returned he, "they lie too deep for discovery" (laying his hand upon his bosom); "they remain buried, riveted here."

After he was gone, upon a general consultation, we could not tell what to make of these fine sentiments. Olivia considered them as instances of the most exalted passion; but I was not quite so sanguine: it seemed to me pretty plain, that they had more of love than matrimony in them; yet, whatever they might portend, it was resolved to prosecute the scheme of farmer Williams, who, from my daughter's first appearance in the country, had paid her his addresses.

CHAPTER XVII

As I only studied my child's real happiness, the assiduity of
Mr Williams pleased me, as he was in easy circumstances, prudent, and sincere. It required but very little encouragement to
revive his former passion; so that in an evening or two he and
Mr Thornhill met at our house, and surveyed each other for
some time with looks of anger; but Williams owed his landlord
no rent, and little regarded his indignation. Olivia, on her side,
acted the coquette to perfection, if that might be called acting
which was her real character, pretending to lavish all her tenderness on her new lover. Mr Thornhill appeared quite dejected at
this preference, and with a pensive air took leave, though I own
it puzzled me to find him in so much pain as he appeared to be,
when he had it in his power so easily to remove the cause, by
declaring an honourable passion. But whatever uneasiness he
seemed to endure, it could easily be perceived that Olivia's
anguish was still greater. After any of these interviews between
her lovers, of which there were several, she usually retired to
solitude, and there indulged her grief. It was in such a situation

I found her one evening, after she had been for some time supporting a fictitious gaiety. "You now see, my child," said I, "that your confidence in Mr Thornhill's passion was all a dream: he permits the rivalry of another, every way his inferior, though he knows it lies in his power to secure you to himself by a candid declaration."—"Yes, papa," returned she; "but he has his reasons for this delay: I know he has. The sincerity of his looks and words convinces me of his real esteem. A short time, I hope, will discover the generosity of his sentiments, and convince you that my opinion of him has been more just than yours."—"Olivia, my darling," returned I, "every scheme that has been hitherto pursued to compel him to a declaration has been proposed and planned by yourself; nor can you in the least say that I have constrained you. But you must not suppose, my dear, that I will ever be instrumental in suffering his honest rival to be the dupe of your ill-placed passion. Whatever time you require to bring your fancied admirer to an explanation shall be granted; but at the expiration of that term, if he is still regardless, I must absolutely insist that honest Mr Williams shall be rewarded for his fidelity. The character which I have hitherto supported in life demands this from me, and my tenderness as a parent shall never influence my integrity as a man. Name, then, your day; let it be as distant as you think proper; and in the meantime, take care to let Mr Thornhill know the exact time on which I design delivering you up to another. If he really loves you, his own good sense will readily suggest that there is but one method alone to prevent his losing you for ever." This proposal, which she could not avoid considering as perfectly just, was readily agreed to. She again renewed her most positive promise of marrying Mr Williams, in case of the other's insensibility; and at the next opportunity, in Mr Thornhill's presence, that day month was fixed upon for her nuptials with his rival.

Such vigorous proceedings seemed to redouble Mr Thornhill's anxiety: but what Olivia really felt gave me some uneasiness. In this struggle between prudence and passion, her vivacity quite forsook her, and every opportunity of solitude was sought, and spent in tears. One week passed away; but Mr Thornhill made no efforts to restrain her nuptials. The succeeding week he was still assiduous; but not more open. On the third he discontinued his visits entirely, and instead of my daughter testifying any impatience, as I expected, she seemed to retain a pensive tranquillity, which I looked upon as resignation. For my own part, I was now sincerely pleased with thinking that my child was going to be secured in a continuance of competence and peace, and frequently applauded her resolution in preferring happiness to ostentation.

It was within about four days of her intended nuptials, that my little family at night were gathered round a charming fire, telling stories of the past, and laying schemes for the future: busied in forming a thousand projects, and laughing at whatever folly came uppermost. "Well, Moses," cried I, "we shall soon, my boy, have a wedding in the family: what is your opinion of matters and things in general?"—"My opinion, father, is, that all things go on very well: and I was just now thinking, that when sister Livy is married to farmer Williams, we shall then have the loan of his cider-press and brewing-tubs for nothing."—"That we shall, Moses," cried I, "and he will sing us *Death and the Lady,* to raise our spirits into the bargain."—"He has taught that song to our Dick," cried Moses; "and I think he goes through it very prettily."—"Does he so?" cried I; "then let us have it: where's little Dick? let him up with it boldly."—"My brother Dick," cried Bill, my youngest, "is just gone out with sister Livy: but Mr Williams has taught me two songs, and I'll sing them for you, papa. Which song do you choose, *The Dying*

Swan, or the *Elegy on the Death of a Mad Dog?*"—"The elegy, child, by all means," said I; "I never heard that yet: and Deborah, my life, grief, you know, is dry; let us have a bottle of the best gooseberry wine, to keep up our spirits. I have wept so much at all sorts of elegies of late, that without an enlivening glass I am sure this will overcome me; and Sophy, love, take your guitar, and thrum in with the boy a little."

AN ELEGY ON THE DEATH OF A MAD DOG

Good people all, of every sort,
　　Give ear unto my song,
And if you find it wondrous short,
　　It cannot hold you long.

In Islington there was a man,
　　Of whom the world might say,
That still a godly race he ran,
　　Whene'er he went to pray.

A kind and gentle heart he had,
　　To comfort friends and foes;
The naked every day he clad,
　　When he put on his clothes.

And in that town a dog was found,
　　As many dogs there be,
Both mongrel, puppy, whelp, and hound,
　　And curs of low degree.

This dog and man at first were friends;
　　But when a pique began,
The dog, to gain some private ends,
　　Went mad, and bit the man.

Around from all the neighbouring streets
　　The wond'ring neighbours ran,
And swore the dog had lost his wits,
　　To bite so good a man.

90

The wound it seemed both sore and sad
   To every Christian eye;
And while they swore the dog was mad,
   They swore the man would die.

But soon a wonder came to light,
   That showed the rogues they lied:
The man recovered of the bite—
   The dog it was that died.

"A very good boy, Bill, upon my word; and an elegy that may truly be called tragical. Come, my children, here's Bill's health, and may he one day be a bishop!"

"With all my heart," cried my wife; "and if he but preaches as well as he sings, I make no doubt of him. The most of his family, by the mother's side, could sing a good song: it was a common saying in our country, that the family of the Blenkinsops could never look straight before them, nor the Hugginsons blow out a candle; that there were none of the Grograms but could sing a song, or of the Marjorams but could tell a story." —"However that be," cried I, "the most vulgar ballad of them all generally pleases me better than the fine modern odes, and things that petrify us in a single stanza—productions that we at once detest and praise.—Put the glass to your brother, Moses.— The great fault of these elegiasts is, that they are in despair for griefs that give the sensible part of mankind very little pain. A lady loses her muff, her fan, or her lap-dog, and so the silly poet runs home to versify the disaster."

"That may be the mode," cried Moses, "in sublimer compositions: but the Ranelagh songs that come down to us are perfectly familiar, and all cast in the same mould: Colin meets Dolly, and they hold a dialogue together; he gives her a fairing to put in her hair, and she presents him with a nosegay; and then they go together to church, where they give good advice

91

to young nymphs and swains to get married as fast as they can."

"And very good advice, too," cried I; "and I am told there is not a place in the world where advice can be given with so much propriety as there: for as it persuades us to marry, it also furnishes us with a wife; and surely that must be an excellent market, my boy, where we are told what we want, and supplied with it when wanting."

"Yes, Sir," returned Moses, "and I know but of two such markets for wives in Europe,—Ranelagh in England, and Font-arabia in Spain. The Spanish market is open once a year; but our English wives are saleable every night."

"You are right, my boy," cried his mother; "Old England is the only place in the world for husbands to get wives."—"And for wives to manage their husbands," interrupted I. "It is a proverb abroad, that if a bridge were built across the sea, all the ladies of the Continent would come over to take pattern with ours; for there are no such wives in Europe as our own. But let us have one bottle more, Deborah, my life; and, Moses, give us a good song. What thanks do we not owe to Heaven for thus bestowing tranquillity, health and competence! I think myself happier now than the greatest monarch upon earth. He has no such fireside, nor such pleasant faces about it. Yes, Deborah, we are now growing old; but the evening of our life is likely to be happy. We are descended from ancestors that knew no stain, and we shall leave a good and virtuous race of children behind us. While we live, they will be our support and our pleasure here: and when we die, they will transmit our honour untainted to posterity. Come, my son, we wait for a song: let us have a chorus. But where is my darling Olivia? that little cherub's voice is always sweetest in the concert." Just as I spoke Dick came running in. "O papa, papa, she is gone from us, she is gone from us; my sister Livy is gone from us for ever!"—"Gone, child!"—

92

OLIVIA ELOPES

"Yes, she is gone off with two gentlemen in a post-chaise, and one of them kissed her, and said he would die for her: and she cried very much, and was for coming back; but he persuaded her again, and she went into the chaise, and said, 'Oh, what will my poor papa do when he knows I am undone!' "—"Now, then," cried I, "my children, go and be miserable; for we shall never enjoy one hour more. And oh, may Heaven's everlasting fury light upon him and his!—thus to rob me of my child! And sure it will, for taking back my sweet innocent that I was leading up to Heaven. Such sincerity as my child was possessed of! But all our earthly happiness is now over! Go, my children, go and be miserable and infamous; for my heart is broken within me!"— "Father," cried my son, "is this your fortitude?"—"Fortitude, child? yes, he shall see I have fortitude! Bring me my pistols. I'll pursue the traitor—while he is on earth I'll pursue him. Old as I am, he shall find I can sting him yet. The villain, the perfidious villain!" I had by this time reached down my pistols, when my poor wife, whose passions were not so strong as mine, caught me in her arms. "My dearest, dearest husband!" cried she, "the Bible is the only weapon that is fit for your old hands now. Open that, my love, and read our anguish into patience, for she has vilely deceived us."—"Indeed, Sir," resumed my son, after a pause, "your rage is too violent and unbecoming. You should be my mother's comforter, and you increase her pain. It ill suited you and your reverend character thus to curse your greatest enemy: you should not have cursed him, villain as he is."—"I did not curse him, child, did I?"—"Indeed, Sir, you did; you cursed him twice."—"Then may Heaven forgive me and him if I did! And now, my son, I see it was more than human benevolence that first taught us to bless our enemies: Blessed be His holy name for all the good He hath given, and for all that He hath taken away. But it is not—it is not a small distress that can wring tears from these old eyes, that have not wept for so many years. My child! to undo my darling!—May confusion seize—— Heaven forgive me! what am I about to say!—You may remember, my love, how good she was, and how charming: till this vile moment all her care was to make us happy. Had she but died! But she is gone, the honour of our family contaminated, and I must look out for happiness in other worlds than here. But, my child, you saw them go off: perhaps he forced her away? If he forced her, she may yet be innocent."—"Ah, no, sir," cried the child; "he only kissed her, and called her his angel, and she wept very much, and leaned upon his arm, and they drove off very fast."—"She's an ungrateful creature," cried my wife, who could scarcely speak for weeping, "to use us thus. She never had the least constraint put upon her affections. The vile strumpet has basely deserted her parents without any provocation, thus to bring your grey hairs to the grave; and I must shortly follow."

In this manner that night, the first of our real misfortunes, was spent in the bitterness of complaint, and ill-supported sallies of enthusiasm. I determined, however, to find out our betrayer, wherever he was, and reproach his baseness. The next morning we missed our wretched child at breakfast, where she used to give life and cheerfulness to us all. My wife, as before, attempted to ease her heart by reproaches. "Never," cried she, "shall that vilest stain of our family again darken these harmless doors. I will never call her daughter more. No, let the strumpet live with her vile seducer: she may bring us to shame, but she shall never more deceive us."

"Wife," said I, "do not talk thus hardly: my detestation of her guilt is as great as yours; but ever shall this house and this heart be open to a poor returning repentant sinner. The sooner she returns from her transgressions, the more welcome shall she be

94

to me. For the first time the very best may err; art may persuade, and novelty spread out its charm. The first fault is the child of simplicity, but every other, the offspring of guilt. Yes, the wretched creature shall be welcome to this heart and this house, though stained with ten thousand vices. I will again hearken to the music of her voice, again will I hang fondly on her bosom, if I find but repentance there. My son, bring hither my Bible and my staff: I will pursue her, wherever she is; and though I cannot save her from shame, I may prevent the continuance of iniquity."

CHAPTER XVIII

Though the child could not describe the gentleman's person who handed his sister into the post-chaise, yet my suspicions fell entirely upon our young landlord, whose character for such intrigues was but too well known. I therefore directed my steps towards Thornhill Castle, resolving to upbraid him, and, if possible, to bring back my daughter: but before I had reached his seat, I was met by one of my parishioners, who said he saw a young lady resembling my daughter in a post-chaise with a gentleman, whom by the description I could only guess to be Mr Burchell, and that they drove very fast. This information, however, did by no means satisfy me. I therefore went to the young 'Squire's, and, though it was yet early, insisted upon seeing him immediately. He soon appeared with the most open familiar air, and seemed perfectly amazed at my daughter's elopement, protesting, upon his honour, that he was quite a stranger to it. I now therefore condemned my former suspicions, and could turn them only on Mr Burchell, who, I recollected, had of late several private conferences with her; but the appearance of another witness left me no room to doubt his villainy, who averred, that he and my daughter were actually gone towards the Wells, about thirty miles off, where there was a great deal of company. Being driven to that state of mind in which we are all more ready to act precipitately than to reason right, I never debated with myself whether these accounts might not have been given by persons purposely placed in my way to mislead me, but resolved to pursue my daughter and her fancied deluder thither. I walked along with earnestness, and inquired of several by the way; but received no accounts, till entering the town, I was met by a person on horseback, whom I remembered to have seen at the 'Squire's, and he assured me that if I followed them to the races, which were about thirty miles farther, I might depend upon overtaking them; for he had seen them dance there the night before, and the whole assembly seemed charmed with my daughter's performance. Early the next day, I walked forward to the races, and about four in the afternoon I came upon the course. The company made a very brilliant appearance, all earnestly employed in one pursuit,—that of pleasure; how different from mine,—that of reclaiming a lost child to virtue! I thought I perceived Mr Burchell at some distance from me; but, as if he dreaded an interview, upon my approaching him he mixed among a crowd, and I saw him no more.

I now reflected that it would be to no purpose to continue my pursuit farther, and resolved to return home to an innocent family, who wanted my assistance. But the agitations of my mind, and the fatigues I had undergone, threw me into a fever, the symptoms of which I perceived before I came off the course. This was another unexpected stroke, as I was more than seventy miles distant from home: however, I retired to a little alehouse by the road-side; and in this place, the usual retreat of indigence and frugality, I laid me down patiently to wait the issue of my disorder. I languished here for near three weeks; but at last my constitution prevailed, though I was unprovided with money to defray the expenses of my entertainment. It is possible the anxiety from this last circumstance alone might have brought on a relapse, had I not been supplied by a traveller, who stopped to take a cursory refreshment. This person was no other than the philanthropic bookseller in St Paul's Churchyard, who has written so many little books for children: he called himself their friend, but he was the friend of all mankind. He was no sooner alighted, but he was in haste to be gone; for he was ever on business of the utmost importance, and was at that time actually compiling materials for the history of one Mr Thomas Trip. I immediately recollected this good-natured man's red pimpled face; for he had published for me against the Deuterogamists of the age; from him I borrowed a few pieces, to be paid at my return. Leaving the inn, therefore, as I was yet but weak, I resolved to return home by easy journeys of ten miles a day. My health and usual tranquillity were almost restored, and I now condemned that pride which had made me refractory to the hand of correction. Man little knows what calamities are beyond his patience to bear, till he tries them: as in ascending the heights of ambition, which look bright from below, every step we rise shows us some new and gloomy prospect of hidden disappointment: so in our descent from the summits of pleasure, though the vale of misery below may appear at first dark and gloomy, yet the busy mind, still attentive to its own amusement, finds, as we descend, something to flatter and to please. Still as we approach, the darkest objects appear to brighten, and the mental eye becomes adapted to its gloomy situation.

I now proceeded forward, and had walked about two hours, when I perceived what appeared at a distance like a waggon, which I was resolved to overtake: but when I came up with it, found it to be a strolling company's cart, that was carrying their scenes and other theatrical furniture to the next village, where they were to exhibit. The cart was attended only by the person who drove it, and one of the company, as the rest of the players were to follow the ensuing day. "Good company upon the road," says the proverb, "is the shortest cut." I therefore entered into conversation with the poor player; and as I once had some theatrical powers myself, I dissertated on such topics with my usual freedom: but as I was pretty much unacquainted with the present state of the stage, I demanded who were the present theatrical writers in vogue—who the Drydens and Otways of the day? —"I fancy, Sir," cried the player, "few of our modern dramatists would think themselves much honoured by being compared to the writers you mention. Dryden and Rowe's manners, Sir, are quite out of fashion: our taste has gone back a whole century; Fletcher, Ben Jonson, and all the plays of Shakespeare are the only things that go down."—"How," cried I, "is it possible the present age can be pleased with that antiquated dialect, that obsolete humour, those overcharged characters, which abound in the works you mention?"—"Sir," returned my companion, "the public think nothing about dialect, or humour, or character, for that is none of their business; they only go to be amused, and find themselves happy when they can enjoy a pantomime, under the sanction of Jonson's or Shakespeare's name."—"So then I suppose," cried I, "that our modern dramatists are rather imitators of Shakespeare than of nature."—"To say the truth," returned my companion, "I don't know that they imitate anything at all; nor, indeed, does the public require it of them; it is not the composition of the piece, but the number of starts and attitudes that may be introduced into it, that elicits applause. I have known a piece, with not one jest in the whole, shrugged into popularity, and another saved by the poet's throwing in a

99

fit of the gripes. No, Sir, the works of Congreve and Farquhar have too much wit in them for the present taste; our modern dialect is much more natural."

By this time, the equipage of the strolling company was arrived at the village, which, it seems, had been apprised of our approach, and was come out to gaze at us; for my companion observed, that strollers always have more spectators without doors than within. I did not consider the impropriety of my being in such company, till I saw a mob gather about me. I therefore took shelter, as fast as possible, in the first alehouse that offered; and being shown into the common room, was accosted by a well-dressed gentleman, who demanded whether I was the real chaplain of the company, or whether it was only to be my masquerade character in the play? Upon informing him of the truth, and that I did not belong, in any sort, to the company, he was condescending enough to desire me and the player to partake in a bowl of punch, over which he discussed modern politics with great earnestness and interest. I set him down, in my own mind, for nothing less than a parliament-man at least; but was almost confirmed in my conjectures, when, upon asking what there was in the house for supper, he insisted that the player and I should sup with him at his house; with which request, after some entreaties, we were prevailed on to comply.

CHAPTER XIX

THE house where we were to be entertained lying at a small distance from the village, our inviter observed, that as the coach was not ready, he would conduct us on foot; and we soon arrived at one of the most magnificent mansions I had seen in that part of the country. The apartment into which we were shown was perfectly elegant and modern: he went to give orders for supper, while the player, with a wink, observed that we were perfectly in luck. Our entertainer soon returned; an elegant supper was brought in; two or three ladies in easy dishabille were introduced, and the conversation began with some sprightliness. Politics, however, were the subject on which our entertainer chiefly expatiated; for he asserted that liberty was at once his boast and his terror. After the cloth was removed, he asked me if I had seen the last *Monitor?* to which, replying in the negative, "What! nor the *Auditor,* I suppose?" cried he. "Neither, Sir," returned I. "That's strange, very strange!" replied my entertainer. "Now, I read all the politics that come out: the *Daily,* the *Public,* the *Ledger,* the *Chronicle,* the *London Evening,* the

Whitehall Evening, the seventeen Magazines, and the two Reviews; and, though they hate each other, I love them all. Liberty, Sir, liberty is the Briton's boast! and, by all my coal-mines in Cornwall, I reverence its guardians."—"Then, it is to be hoped," cried I, "you reverence the king?"—"Yes," returned my entertainer, "when he does what we would have him; but if he goes on as he has done of late, I'll never trouble myself more with his matters. I say nothing. I think only. I could have directed some things better. I don't think there has been a sufficent number of advisers: he should advise with every person willing to give him advice, and then we should have things done in another-guess manner."

"I wish," cried I, "that such intruding advisers were fixed in the pillory. It should be the duty of honest men to assist the weaker side of our constitution, that sacred power that has for some years been every day declining, and losing its due share of influence in the State. But these ignorants still continue the same cry of liberty, and, if they have any weight, basely throw it into the subsiding scale."

"How!" cried one of the ladies, "do I live to see one so base, so sordid, as to be an enemy to liberty, and a defender of tyrants? Liberty, that sacred gift of Heaven, that glorious privilege of Britons!"

"Can it be possible," cried our entertainer, "that there should be any found at present advocates for slavery? Any who are for meanly giving up the privileges of Britons? Can any, Sir, be so abject?"

"No, Sir," replied I, "I am for liberty! that attribute of gods! Glorious liberty! that theme of modern declamation! I would have all men kings! I would be a king myself. We have all naturally an equal right to the throne: we are all originally equal. This is my opinion, and was once the opinion of a set of honest

102

men who were called Levellers. They tried to erect themselves into a community, where all should be equally free. But, alas! it would never answer: for there were some among them stronger, and some more cunning, than others, and these became masters of the rest: for, as sure as your groom rides your horses, because he is a cunninger animal than they, so surely will the animal that is cunninger or stronger than he, sit upon his shoulders in turn. Since, then, it is entailed upon humanity to submit, and some are born to command and other to obey, the question is, as there must be tyrants, whether it is better to have them in the same house with us, or in the same village, or, still farther off, in the metropolis. Now, Sir, for my own part, as I naturally hate the face of a tyrant, the farther off he is removed from me the better pleased am I. The generality of mankind also are of my way of thinking, and have unanimously created one king, whose election at once diminishes the number of tyrants, and puts tyranny at the greatest distance from the greatest number of people. Now the great, who were tyrants themselves before the election of one tyrant, are naturally averse to a power raised over them, and whose weight must ever lean heaviest on the subordinate orders. It is the interest of the great, therefore, to diminish kingly power as much as possible; because, whatever they take from that is naturally restored to themselves; and all they have to do in the state is to undermine the single tyrant, by which they resume their primeval authority. Now the state may be so circumstanced, or its laws may be so disposed, or its men of opulence so minded, as all to conspire in carrying on this business of undermining monarchy. For, in the first place, if the circumstances of our state be such as to favour the accumulation of wealth, and make the opulent still more rich, this will increase their ambition. An accumulation of wealth, however, must necessarily be the consequence, when, as at present, more riches flow in from external commerce than arise from internal industry; for external commerce can only be managed to advantage by the rich, and they have also at the same time all the emoluments arising from internal industry; so that the rich, with us, have two sources of wealth, whereas the poor have but one. For this reason, wealth, in all commercial states, is found to accumulate; and all such have hitherto in time become aristocratical. Again, the very laws also of this country may contribute to the accumulation of wealth; as when, by their means, the natural ties that bind the rich and poor together are broken, and it is ordained that the rich shall only marry with the rich; or when the learned are held unqualified to serve their country as counsellors, merely from a defect of opulence, and wealth is thus made the object of a wise man's ambition: by these means, I say, and such means as these, riches will accumulate. Now, the possessor of accumulated wealth, when furnished with the necessaries and pleasures of life, has no other method to employ the superfluity of his fortune but in purchasing power. That is, differently speaking, in making dependants, by purchasing the liberty of the needy or the venal, of men who are willing to bear the mortification of contiguous tyranny for bread. Thus each very opulent man generally gathers round him a circle of the poorest of the people; and the polity abounding in accumulated wealth may be compared to a Cartesian system, each orb with a vortex of his own. Those, however, who are willing to move in a great man's vortex, are only such as must be slaves, the rabble of mankind, whose souls and whose education are adapted to servitude, and who know nothing of liberty except the name. But there must still be a large number of the people without the sphere of the opulent man's influence; namely, that order of men which subsists between the very rich and the very rabble; those men who are possessed of too large fortunes to submit to the

104

neighbouring man in power, and yet are too poor to set up for tyranny themselves. In this middle order of mankind are generally to be found all the arts, wisdom, and virtues of society. This order alone is known to be the true preserver of freedom, and may be called THE PEOPLE. Now, it may happen that this middle order of mankind may lose all its influence in a state, and its voice be in a manner drowned in that of the rabble: for if the fortune sufficient for qualifying a person at present to give his voice in state affairs be ten times less than was judged sufficient upon forming the constitution, it is evident that great numbers of the rabble will thus be introduced into the political system, and they, ever moving in the vortex of the great, will follow where greatness shall direct. In such a state, therefore, all that the middle order has left, is to preserve the prerogative and privileges of the one principal governor with the most sacred circumspection. For he divides the power of the rich, and calls off the great from falling with tenfold weight on the middle order placed beneath them. The middle order may be compared to a town of which the opulent are forming the siege, and of which the governor from without is hastening the relief. While the besiegers are in dread of an enemy over them, it is but natural to offer the townsmen the most specious terms; to flatter them with sounds, and amuse them with privileges; but if they once defeat the governor from behind, the walls of the town will be but a small defence to its inhabitants. What they may then expect, may be seen by turning our eyes to Holland, Genoa, or Venice, where the laws govern the poor, and the rich govern the law. I am then for, and would die for, monarchy, sacred monarchy: for if there be anything sacred amongst men, it must be the anointed SOVEREIGN of his people; and every diminution of his power, in war or in peace, is an infringement upon the real liberties of the subject. The sounds of Liberty, Patriotism, and

Britons, have already done much; it is to be hoped that the true sons of freedom will prevent their ever doing more. I have known many of those pretended champions for liberty in my time, yet do I not remember one that was not in his heart and in his family a tyrant."

My warmth, I found, had lengthened this harangue beyond the rules of good breeding; but the impatience of my entertainer, who often strove to interrupt it, could be restrained no longer. "What!" cried he, "then I have been all this while entertaining a Jesuit in parson's clothes! But, by all the coal-mines of Cornwall, out he shall pack, if my name be Wilkinson." I now found I had gone too far, and asked pardon for the warmth with which I had spoken. "Pardon!" returned he in a fury: "I think such principles demand ten thousand pardons. What! give up liberty, property, and as the *Gazetteer* says, lie down to be saddled with wooden shoes! Sir, I insist upon your marching out of this house immediately, to prevent worse consequences: sir, I insist upon it." I was going to repeat my remonstrances, but just then we heard a footman's rap at the door, and the two ladies cried out, "As sure as death, there is our master and mistress come home!" It seems my entertainer was all this while only the butler, who, in his master's absence, had a mind to cut a figure, and be for a while the gentleman himself; and, to say the truth, he talked politics as well as most country gentlemen do. But nothing could now exceed my confusion upon seeing the gentleman and his lady enter; nor was their surprise, at finding such company and good cheer, less than ours. "Gentlemen," cried the real master of the house to me and my companion, "my wife and I are your most humble servants; but I protest this is so unexpected a favour, that we almost sink under the obligation." However unexpected our company might be to them, theirs, I am sure, was still more so to us, and I was struck dumb with the apprehension

THE VICAR FINDS HIS SON

of my own absurdity, when whom should I next see enter the room but my dear Miss Arabella Wilmot, who was formerly designed to be married to my son George, but whose match was broken off, as already related. As soon as she saw me, she flew to my arms with the utmost joy. "My dear sir," cried she, "to what happy accident is it that we owe so unexpected a visit? I am sure my uncle and aunt will be in raptures when they find they have the good Dr Primrose for their guest." Upon hearing my name, the old gentleman and lady very politely stepped up, and welcomed me with most cordial hospitality. Nor could they forbear smiling, upon being informed of the nature of my present visit: but the unfortunate butler, whom they at first seemed disposed to turn away, was at my intercession forgiven.

Mr Arnold and his lady, to whom the house belonged, now insisted upon having the pleasure of my stay for some days; and as their niece, my charming pupil, whose mind in some measure had been formed under my own instructions, joined in their entreaties, I complied. That night I was shown to a magnificent chamber; and the next morning early Miss Wilmot desired to walk with me in the garden, which was decorated in the modern manner. After some time spent in pointing out the beauties of the place, she inquired, with seeming unconcern, when last I had heard from my son George.—"Alas! madam," cried I, "he has now been nearly three years absent, without ever writing to his friends or me. Where he is I know not; perhaps I shall never see him or happiness more. No, my dear madam, we shall never more see such pleasing hours as were once spent by our fireside at Wakefield. My little family are now dispersing very fast, and poverty has brought not only want, but infamy upon us." The good-natured girl let fall a tear at this account; but as I saw her possessed of too much sensibility, I forbore a more minute detail of our sufferings. It was, however, some consolation to me to find that time had made no alteration in her affections, and that she had rejected several matches that had been made her since our leaving her part of the country. She led me round all the extensive improvements of the place, pointing to the several walks and arbours, and at the same time catching from every object a hint for some new question relative to my son. In this manner we spent the forenoon, till the bell summoned us in to dinner, where we found the manager of the strolling company that I mentioned before, who was come to dispose of tickets for the *Fair Penitent,* which was to be acted that evening: the part of Horatio by a young gentleman who had never appeared on any stage. He seemed to be very warm in the praises of the new performer, and averred that he never saw any who bid so fair for excellence. Acting, be observed, was not learned in a day; "but this gentleman," continued he, "seems born to tread the stage. His voice, his figure, and attitudes are all admirable. We caught him up accidentally in our journey down." This account in some measure excited our curiosity, and, at the entreaty of the ladies, I was prevailed upon to accompany them to the play-house, which was no other than a barn. As the company with which I went was incontestably the chief of the place, we were received with the greatest respect, and placed in the front seat of the theatre, where we sat for some time with no small impatience to see Horatio make his appearance. The new performer advanced at last; and let parents think of my sensations by their own, when I found it was my unfortunate son! He was going to begin; when, turning his eyes upon the audience, he perceived Miss Wilmot and me, and stood at once speechless and immovable.

The actors behind the scene, who ascribed this pause to his natural timidity, attempted to encourage him; but instead of going on, he burst into a flood of tears, and retired off the stage

108

I don't know what were my feelings on this occasion, for they succeeded with too much rapidity for description; but I was soon awaked from this disagreeable reverie by Miss Wilmot, who, pale, and with a trembling voice, desired me to conduct her back to her uncle's. When got home, Mr Arnold, who was as yet a stranger to our extraordinary behaviour, being informed that the new performer was my son, sent his coach and an invitation for him; and as he persisted in his refusal to appear again upon the stage, the players put another in his place, and we soon had him with us. Mr Arnold gave him the kindest reception, and I received him with my usual transport; for I could never counterfeit false resentment. Miss Wilmot's reception was mixed with seeming neglect, and yet I could perceive she acted a studied part. The tumult in her mind seemed not yet abated: she said twenty giddy things that looked like joy, and then laughed loud at her own want of meaning. At intervals she would take a sly peep at the glass, as if happy in the consciousness of unresisted beauty; and often would ask questions, without giving any manner of attention to the answers.

CHAPTER XX

After we had supped, Mrs Arnold politely offered to send a couple of her footmen for my son's baggage, which he at first seemed to decline; but upon her pressing the request, he was obliged to inform her, that a stick and wallet were all the movable things upon this earth that he could boast of. "Why, ay, my son," cried I, "you left me but poor, and poor I find you are come back: and yet I make no doubt you have seen a great deal of the world."—"Yes, Sir," replied my son, "but travelling after Fortune is not the way to secure her; and, indeed, of late I have desisted from the pursuit."—"I fancy, Sir," cried Mrs Arnold, "that the account of your adventures would be amusing; the first part of them I have often heard from my niece; but could the company prevail for the rest, it would be an additional obligation."—"Madam," replied my son, "I promise you the pleasure you have in hearing will not be half so great as my vanity in repeating them; yet in the whole narrative I can scarcely promise you one adventure, as my account is rather of what I saw than what I did. The first misfortune of my life, which you all

110

know, was great; but though it distressed, it could not sink me. No person ever had a better knack at hoping than I. The less kind I found Fortune at one time, the more I expected from her another; and being now at the bottom of her wheel, every new revolution might lift, but could not depress me. I proceeded, therefore, towards London in a fine morning, no way uneasy about to-morrow, but cheerful as the birds that carolled by the road; and comforted myself with reflecting, that London was the mart where abilities of every kind were sure of meeting distinction and reward.

"Upon my arrival in town, Sir, my first care was to deliver your letter of recommendation to our cousin, who was himself in little better circumstances than I. My first scheme, you know, Sir, was to be usher at an academy; and I asked his advice on the affair. Our cousin received the proposal with a true sardonic grin. 'Ay,' cried he, 'this is indeed a very pretty career that has been chalked out for you. I have been an usher at a boarding-school myself; and may I die by an anodyne necklace, but I had rather be an under-turnkey in Newgate. I was up early and late: I was browbeat by the master, hated for my ugly face by the mistress, worried by the boys within, and never permitted to stir out to meet civility abroad. But are you sure you are fit for a school? Let me examine you a little. Have you been bred apprentice to the business?'—'No.'—'Then you won't do for a school. Can you dress the boys' hair?'—'No.'—'Then you won't do for a school. Have you had the smallpox?'—'No.'—'Then you won't do for a school. Can you lie three in a bed?'—'No.'—'Then you will never do for a school. Have you got a good stomach?'— 'Yes.'—'Then you will by no means do for a school. No, sir: if you are for a genteel, easy profession, bind yourself seven years an apprentice to turn a cutler's wheel; but avoid a school by any means. Yet, come,' continued he, 'I see you are a lad of spirit

111

and learning; what do you think of commencing author like me? You have read in books, no doubt, of men of genius starving at the trade. At present I'll show you forty very dull fellows about town that live by it in opulence; all honest, jog-trot men, who go on smoothly and dully, and write history and politics, and are praised—men, Sir, who, had they been bred cobblers, would all their lives have only mended shoes, but never made them.'

"Finding that there was no great degree of gentility affixed to the character of an usher, I resolved to accept his proposal; and having the highest respect for literature, hailed the *antiqua mater* of Grub Street with reverence. I thought it my glory to pursue a track which Dryden and Otway trod before me. I considered the goddess of this region as the parent of excellence; and however an intercourse with the world might give us good sense, the poverty she granted I supposed to be the nurse of genius! Big with these reflections, I sat down, and finding that the best things remained to be said on the wrong side, I resolved to write a book that should be wholly new. I therefore dressed up three paradoxes with some ingenuity. They were false, indeed, but they were new. The jewels of truth have been so often imported by others, that nothing was left for me to import but some splendid things that at a distance looked every bit as well. Witness, you powers, what fancied importance sat perched upon my quill while I was writing! The whole learned world, I made no doubt, would rise to oppose my systems; but then I was prepared to oppose the whole learned world. Like the porcupine, I sat self-collected, with a quill pointed against every opposer."

"Well said, my boy," cried I; "and what subject did you treat upon? I hope you did not pass over the importance of monogamy. But I interrupt: go on. You published your paradoxes; well, and what did the learned world say to your paradoxes?"

"Sir," replied my son, "the learned world said nothing to my paradoxes; nothing at all, Sir. Every man of them was employed in praising his friends or himself, and condemning his enemies; and unfortunately, as I had neither, I suffered the cruellest mortification—neglect.

"As I was meditating one day in a coffee-house on the fate of my paradoxes, a little man, happening to enter the room, placed himself in the box before me, and after some preliminary discourse, finding me to be a scholar, drew out a bundle of proposals, begging me to subscribe to a new edition he was going to give to the world of Propertius, with Notes. This demand necessarily produced a reply that I had no money; and that concession led him to inquire into the nature of my expectations. Finding that my expectations were just as great as my purse— 'I see,' cried he, 'you are unacquainted with the town: I'll teach you a part of it. Look at these proposals,—upon these very proposals I have subsisted very comfortably for twelve years. The moment a nobleman returns from his travels, a Creolian arrives from Jamaica, or a dowager from her country seat, I strike for a subscription. I first besiege their hearts with flattery, and then pour in my proposals at the breach. If they subscribe readily the first time, I renew my request to beg a dedication fee. If they let me have that, I smite them once more for engraving their coat-of-arms at the top. Thus,' continued he, 'I live by vanity, and laugh at it. But, between ourselves, I am now too well known; I should be glad to borrow your face a bit. A nobleman of distinction has just returned from Italy; my face is familiar to his porter; but if you bring this copy of verses, my life for it you succeed, and we divide the spoil.' "

"Bless us, George," cried I, "and is this the employment of poets now? Do men of their exalted talents thus stoop to beggary? Can they so far disgrace their calling as to make a vile traffic of praise for bread?"

113

"Oh no, Sir," returned he, "a true poet can never be so base; for wherever there is genius, there is pride. The creatures I now describe are only beggars in rhyme. The real poet, as he braves every hardship for fame, so he is equally a coward to contempt; and none but those who are unworthy protection, condescend to solicit it.

"Having a mind too proud to stoop to such indignities, and yet a fortune too humble to hazard a second attempt for fame, I was now obliged to take a middle course, and write for bread. But I was unqualified for a profession where mere industry alone was to ensure success. I could not suppress my lurking passion for applause; but usually consumed that time in efforts after excellence which takes up but little room, when it should have been more advantageously employed in the diffusive productions of fruitful mediocrity. My little piece would therefore come forth in the midst of periodical publications, unnoticed and unknown. The public were more importantly employed than to observe the easy simplicity of my style or the harmony of my periods. Sheet after sheet was thrown off to oblivion. My essays were buried among the essays upon liberty, Eastern tales, and cures for the bite of a mad dog; while Philautos, Philalethes, Philelutheros, and Philanthropos all wrote better, because they wrote faster than I.

"Now, therefore, I began to associate with none but disappointed authors like myself, who praised, deplored, and despised each other. The satisfaction we found in every celebrated writer's attempts was inversely as their merits. I found that no genius in another could please me. My unfortunate paradoxes had entirely dried up that source of comfort. I could neither read nor write with satisfaction; for excellence in another was my aversion, and writing was my trade.

"In the midst of these gloomy reflections, as I was one day

114

sitting on a bench in St James's Park, a young gentleman of distinction, who had been my intimate acquaintance at the university, approached me. We saluted each other with some hesitation; he almost ashamed of being known to one who made so shabby an appearance, and I afraid of repulse. But my suspicions soon vanished; for Ned Thornhill was at the bottom a very good-natured fellow."

"What did you say, George?" interrupted I. "Thornhill—was not that his name? It can certainly be no other than my landlord."—"Bless me," cried Mrs Arnold, "is Mr Thornhill so near a neighbour of yours? He has long been a friend in our family, and we expect a visit from him shortly."

"My friend's first care," continued my son, "was to alter my appearance by a very fine suit of his own clothes, and then I was admitted to his table, upon the footing of half friend, half underling. My business was to attend him at auctions, to put him in spirits when he sat for his picture, to take the left hand in his chariot when not filled by another, and to assist at tattering a kip, as the phrase was when he had a mind for a frolic. Besides this, I had twenty other little employments in the family. I was to do many small things without bidding: to carry the corkscrew; to stand godfather to all the butler's children; to sing when I was bid; to be never out of humour; always to be humble, and, if I could, to be very happy.

"In this honourable post, however, I was not without a rival. A captain of marines, who was formed for the place by nature, opposed me in my patron's affections. His mother had been laundress to a man of quality, and thus he early acquired a taste for pimping and pedigree. As this gentleman made it the study of his life to be acquainted with lords, though he was dismissed from several for his stupidity, yet he found many of them, who were as dull as himself, that permitted his assiduities. As flattery was his trade, he practised it with the easiest address imaginable; but it came awkward and stiff from me; and as every day my patron's desire of flattery increased, so every hour, being better acquainted with his defects, I became more unwilling to give it. Thus, I was once more fairly going to give the field to the captain, when my friend found occasion for my assistance. This was nothing less than to fight a duel for him with a gentleman whose sister it was pretended he had used ill. I readily complied with this request; and though I see you are displeased at my conduct, yet, as it was a debt indispensably due to friendship, I could not refuse. I undertook the affair, disarmed my antagonist, and soon after had the pleasure of finding that the lady was only a woman of the town, and the fellow her bully and a sharper. This piece of service was repaid with the warmest professions of gratitude; but, as my friend was to leave town in a few days, he knew no other method of serving me but by recommending me to his uncle, Sir William Thornhill, and another nobleman of great distinction, who enjoyed a post under the government. When he was gone, my first care was to carry his recommendatory letter to his uncle, a man whose character for every virtue was universal, yet just. I was received by his servants with the most hospitable smiles; for the looks of the domestic ever transmit the master's benevolence. Being shown into a grand apartment, where Sir William soon came to me, I delivered my message and letter, which he read, and after pausing some minutes—'Pray, Sir,' cried he, 'inform me what you have done for my kinsman, to deserve this warm recommendation? But I suppose, Sir, I guess your merits: you have fought for him: and so you would expect a reward from me for being the instrument of his vices. I wish—sincerely wish—that my present refusal may be some punishment for your guilt; but still more, that it may be some inducement to your repentance.' The severity of this rebuke I bore patiently, because I knew it was just. My whole expectations now, therefore, lay in my letter to the great man. As the doors of the nobility are almost ever beset with beggars, all ready to thrust in some sly petition, I found it no easy matter to gain admittance. However, after bribing the servants with half my worldly fortune, I was at last shown into a spacious apartment, my letter being previously sent up for his lordship's inspection. During this anxious interval I had full time to look round me. Everything was grand and of happy contrivance; the paintings, the furniture, the gildings, petrified me with awe, and raised my idea of the owner. Ah, thought I to myself, how very great must the possessor of all these things be, who carries in his head the business of the state, and whose house displays half the wealth of a kingdom! Sure his genius must be unfathomable! During these awful reflections I heard a step come heavily forward. Ah, this is the great man himself! No; it was only a chamber-maid. Another foot was heard soon after. This must be He! No; it was only the great man's valet-de-chambre. At last his lordship actually made his appearance. 'Are you,' cried he, 'the bearer of this here letter?' I answered with a bow. 'I learn by this,' continued he, 'as how that——' But just at that instant a servant delivered him a card, and without taking further notice, he went out of the room, and left me to digest my own happiness at leisure. I saw no more of him, till told by a footman that his lordship was going to his coach at the door. Down I immediately followed, and joined my voice to that of three or four more, who came, like me, to petition for favours. His lordship, however, went too fast for us, and was gaining his chariot door with large strides, when I hallooed out to know if I was to have any reply. He was by this time got in, and muttered an answer, half of which only I heard; the other half was lost in the rattling of his chariot wheels. I stood for

117

some time with my neck stretched out, in the posture of one that was listening to catch the glorious sounds, till, looking round me, I found myself alone at his lordship's gate.

"My patience," continued my son, "was now quite exhausted. Stung with the thousand indignities I had met with, I was willing to cast myself away, and only wanted the gulf to receive me. I regarded myself as one of those vile things that Nature designed should be thrown by into her lumber-room, there to perish in obscurity. I had still, however, half a guinea left, and of that I thought Nature herself should not deprive me; but in order to be sure of this, I was resolved to go instantly and spend it while I had it, and then trust to occurrences for the rest. As I was going along with this resolution, it happened that Mr Crispe's office seemed invitingly open to give me a welcome reception. In this office Mr Crispe kindly offers all His Majesty's subjects a generous promise of £30 a year, for which promise all they give in return is their liberty for life, and permission to let him transport them to America as slaves. I was happy at finding a place where I could lose my fears in desperation, and entered this cell (for it had the appearance of one) with the devotion of a monastic. Here I found a number of poor creatures, all in circumstances like myself, expecting the arrival of Mr Crispe, presenting a true epitome of English impatience. Each untractable soul, at variance with Fortune, wreaked her injuries on their own hearts; but Mr Crispe at last came down, and all our murmurs were hushed. He deigned to regard me with an air of peculiar approbation, and indeed he was the first man who, for a month past, had talked to me with smiles. After a few questions, he found I was fit for everything in the world. He paused awhile upon the properest means of providing for me; and slapping his forehead as if he had found it, assured me that there was at that time an embassy talked of from the synod of Pennsylvania to the Chickasaw Indians, and that he would use his interest to get me made secretary. I knew in my own heart that the fellow lied, and yet his promise gave me pleasure, there was something so magnificent in the sound. I fairly, therefore, divided my half-guinea, one half of which went to be added to his thirty thousand pounds, and with the other half I resolved to go to the next tavern, to be there more happy than he.

"As I was going out with that resolution, I was met at the door by the captain of a ship with whom I had formerly some little acquaintance, and he agreed to be my companion over a bowl of punch. As I never chose to make a secret of my circumstances, he assured me that I was upon the very point of ruin, in listening to the office-keeper's promises; for that he only designed to sell me to the plantations. 'But,' continued he, 'I fancy you might, by a much shorter voyage, be very easily put into a genteel way of bread. Take my advice. My ship sails to-morrow for Amsterdam: what if you go in her as a passenger? The moment you land, all you have to do is to teach the Dutchmen English, and I'll warrant you'll get pupils and money enough. I suppose you understand English,' added he, 'by this time, or the deuce is in it.' I confidently assured him of that; but expressed a doubt whether the Dutch would be willing to learn English. He affirmed, with an oath, that they were fond of it to distraction; and upon that affirmation I agreed with his proposal, and embarked the next day to teach the Dutch English in Holland. The wind was fair, our voyage short; and after having paid my passage with half my movables, I found myself fallen as from the skies, a stranger in one of the principal streets of Amsterdam. In this situation I was unwilling to let any time pass unemployed in teaching. I addressed myself, therefore, to two or three of those I met whose appearance seemed most promising; but it was impossible to make ourselves mutually understood.

119

It was not till this very moment I recollected, that in order to teach the Dutchmen English, it was necessary that they should first teach me Dutch. How I came to overlook so obvious an objection is to me amazing: but certain it is I overlooked it.

"This scheme thus blown up, I had some thoughts of fairly shipping back to England again; but happening into company with an Irish student, who was returning from Louvain, our conversation turning upon topics of literature (for, by the way, it may be observed that I always forgot the meanness of my circumstances when I could converse upon such subjects), from him I learned that there were not two men in his whole university who understood Greek. This amazed me. I instantly resolved to travel to Louvain, and there live by teaching Greek: and in this design I was heartened by my brother student, who threw out some hints that a fortune might be got by it.

"I set boldly forward the next morning. Every day lessened the burden of my movables, like Æsop and his basket of bread; for I paid them for my lodgings to the Dutch, as I travelled on. When I came to Louvain, I was resolved not to go sneaking to the lower professors, but openly tendered my talents to the Principal himself. I went, had admittance, and offered him my service as a master of the Greek language, which I had been told was a desideratum in this university. The Principal seemed at first to doubt of my abilities; but of these I offered to convince him, by turning a part of any Greek author he should fix upon into Latin. Finding me perfectly earnest in my proposal, he addressed me thus: 'You see me, young man; I never learned Greek, and I don't find that I have ever missed it. I have had a Doctor's cap and gown without Greek; I have ten thousand florins a year without Greek; I eat heartily without Greek; and, in short,' continued he, 'as I don't know Greek, I do not believe there is any good in it.'

120

"I was now too far from home to think of returning; so I resolved to go forward. I had some knowledge of music, with a tolerable voice, and now turned what was my amusement into a present means of subsistence. I passed among the harmless peasants of Flanders, and among such of the French as were poor enough to be very merry; for I ever found them sprightly in proportion to their wants. Whenever I approached a peasant's house towards night-fall, I played one of my most merry tunes, and that procured me not only a lodging, but subsistence for the next day. I once or twice attempted to play for people of fashion, but they always thought my performance odious, and never rewarded me even with a trifle. This was to me the more extraordinary, as, whenever I used, in better days, to play for company, when playing was my amusement, my music never failed to throw them into raptures, and the ladies especially; but as it was now my only means, it was received with contempt —a proof how ready the world is to underrate those talents by which a man is supported.

"In this manner I proceeded to Paris, with no design but just to look about me, and then to go forward. The people of Paris are much fonder of strangers that have money, than those that have wit. As I could not boast much of either, I was no great favourite. After walking about the town four or five days, and seeing the outsides of the best houses, I was preparing to leave this retreat of venal hospitality, when passing through one of the principal streets, whom should I meet but our cousin, to whom you first recommended me. This meeting was very agreeable to me, and I believe not displeasing to him. He inquired into the nature of my journey to Paris, and informed me of his own business there, which was to collect pictures, medals, intaglios, and antiques of all kinds for a gentleman in London who had just stepped into taste and a large fortune. I was the more

121

surprised at seeing our cousin pitched upon for this office, as he himself had often assured me he knew nothing of the matter. Upon asking how he had been taught the art of a cognoscento so very suddenly, he assured me that nothing was more easy. The whole secret consisted in a strict adherence to two rules: the one, always to observe that the picture might have been better if the painter had taken more pains: and the other, to praise the works of Pietro Perugino. 'But,' says he, 'as I once taught you how to be an author in London, I'll now undertake to instruct you in the art of picture-buying at Paris.'

"With this proposal I very readily closed, as it was living, and now all my ambition was to live. I went therefore to his lodgings, improved my dress by his assistance; and, after some time, accompanied him to auctions of pictures, where the English gentry were expected to be purchasers. I was not a little surprised at his intimacy with people of the best fashion, who referred themselves to his judgment upon every picture or medal, as an unerring standard of taste. He made very good use of my assistance upon these occasions; for, when asked his opinion, he would gravely take me aside and ask mine, shrug, look wise, return, and assure the company that he would give no opinion upon an affair of so much importance. Yet there was sometimes an occasion for a more supported assurance. I remember to have seen him, after giving his opinion that the colouring of a picture was not mellow enough, very deliberately take a brush with brown varnish, that was accidentally lying by, and rub it over the piece with great composure before all the company, and then asked if he had not improved the tints.

"When he had finished his commission in Paris, he left me strongly recommended to several men of distinction, as a person very proper for a travelling tutor; and after some time, I was employed in that capacity by a gentleman who brought his ward

122

to Paris, in order to set him forward on his tour through Europe. I was to be the young gentleman's governor; but with a proviso, that he should always be permitted to govern himself. My pupil, in fact, understood the art of guiding in money concerns much better than I. He was heir to a fortune of about two hundred thousand pounds, left him by an uncle in the West Indies; and his guardians, to qualify him for the management of it, had bound him apprentice to an attorney. Thus avarice was his prevailing passion; all his questions on the road were, how money might be saved; which was the least expensive course of travel; whether anything could be bought that would turn to account when disposed of again in London? Such curiosities on the way as could be seen for nothing, he was ready enough to look at; but if the sight of them was to be paid for, he usually asserted that he had been told they were not worth seeing. He never paid a bill that he would not observe how amazingly expensive travelling was! and all this though he was not yet twenty-one. When arrived at Leghorn, as we took a walk to look at the port and shipping, he inquired the expense of the passage by sea home to England. This he was informed was but a trifle compared to his returning by land; he was therefore unable to withstand the temptation; so paying me the small part of my salary that was due, he took leave, and embarked with only one attendant for London.

"I now therefore was left once more upon the world at large; but then, it was a thing I was used to. However, my skill in music could avail me nothing in a country where every peasant was a better musician than I: but by this time I had acquired another talent, which answered my purpose as well, and this was a skill in disputation. In all the foreign universities and convents there are, upon certain days, philosophical theses maintained against every adventitious disputant; for which, if the champion opposes with any dexterity, he can claim a gratuity in money, a dinner, and a bed for one night. In this manner, therefore, I fought my way towards England; walked along from city to city; examined mankind more nearly; and, if I may so express it, saw both sides of the picture. My remarks, however, are but few: I found that monarchy was the best government for the poor to live in, and commonwealths for the rich. I found that riches in general were in every country another name for freedom; and that no man is so fond of liberty himself as not to be desirous of subjecting the will of some individuals in society to his own.

"Upon my arrival in England, I resolved to pay my respects first to you, and then to enlist as a volunteer in the first expedition that was going forward: but on my journey down, my resolutions were changed by meeting an old acquaintance, who I found belonged to a company of comedians that were going to make a summer campaign in the country. The company seemed not much to disapprove of me for an associate. They all, however, apprised me of the importance of the task at which I aimed; that the public was a many-headed monster, and that only such as had very good heads could please it; that acting was not to be learned in a day; and that without some traditional shrugs, which had been on the stage, and only on the stage, these hundred years, I could never pretend to please. The next difficulty was in fitting me with parts, as almost every character was in keeping. I was driven for some time from one character to another, till at last Horatio was fixed upon, which the presence of the present company has happily hindered me from acting."

CHAPTER XXI

MY son's account was too long to be delivered at once; the first part of it was begun that night, and he was concluding the rest after dinner the next day, when the appearance of Mr Thornhill's equipage at the door seemed to make a pause in the general satisfaction. The butler, who was now become my friend in the family, informed me, with a whisper, that the 'Squire had already made some overtures to Miss Wilmot, and that her aunt and uncle seemed highly to approve the match. Upon Mr Thornhill's entering, he seemed, at seeing my son and me, to start back; but I readily imputed that to surprise, and not displeasure. However, upon our advancing to salute him, he returned our greeting with the most apparent candour; and after a short time his presence served only to increase the general good humour.

After tea he called me aside to inquire after my daughter; but upon my informing him that my inquiry was unsuccessful, he seemed greatly surprised; adding that he had been since frequently at my house in order to comfort the rest of my family, whom he left perfectly well. He then asked if I communicated her misfortune to Miss Wilmot or my son; and upon my replying that I had not told them as yet, he greatly approved my prudence and precaution, desiring me by all means to keep it a secret: "For at best," cried he, "it is but divulging one's own infamy; and perhaps Miss Livy may not be so guilty as we all imagine." We were here interrupted by a servant who came to ask the 'Squire in, to stand up at country dances: so that he left me quite pleased with the interest he seemed to take in my concerns. His addresses, however, to Miss Wilmot were too obvious to be mistaken: and yet, she seemed not perfectly pleased, but bore them rather in compliance to the will of her aunt than from real inclination. I had even the satisfaction to see her lavish some kind looks upon my unfortunate son, which the other could neither extort by his fortune nor assiduity. Mr Thornhill's seeming composure, however, not a little surprised me: we had now continued here a week at the pressing instances of Mr Arnold; but each day the more tenderness Miss Wilmot showed my son, Mr Thornhill's friendship seemed proportionately to increase for him.

He had formerly made us the most kind assurances of using his interest to serve the family; but now his generosity was not confined to promises alone. The morning I designed for my departure, Mr Thornhill came to me with looks of real pleasure, to inform me of a piece of service he had done for his friend George. This was nothing less than his having procured him an ensign's commission in one of the regiments that was going to the West Indies, for which he had promised but one hundred pounds, his interest having been sufficient to get an abatement of the other two. "As for this trifling piece of service," continued the young gentleman, "I desire no other reward but the pleasure of having served my friend; and as for the hundred pounds

126

to be paid, if you are unable to raise it yourselves, I will advance it, and you shall repay me at your leisure." This was a favour we wanted words to express our sense of; I readily, therefore, gave my bond for the money, and testified as much gratitude as if I never intended to pay.

George was to depart for town the next day, to secure his commission, in pursuance of his generous patron's directions, who judged it highly expedient to use despatch, lest in the meantime another should step in with more advantageous proposals. The next morning, therefore, our young soldier was early prepared for his departure, and seemed the only person among us that was not affected by it. Neither the fatigues and dangers he was going to encounter, nor the friends and mistress—for Miss Wilmot actually loved him—he was leaving behind, any way damped his spirits. After he had taken leave of the rest of the company, I gave him all I had, my blessing. "And now, my boy," cried I, "thou art going to fight for thy country; remember how thy brave grandfather fought for his sacred king, when loyalty among Britons was a virtue. Go, my boy, and imitate him in all but his misfortunes, if it was a misfortune to die with Lord Falkland. Go, my boy, and if you fall, though distant, exposed, and unwept by those that love you, the most precious tears are those with which Heaven bedews the unburied head of a soldier."

The next morning I took leave of the good family that had been kind enough to entertain me so long, not without several expressions of gratitude to Mr Thornhill for his late bounty. I left them in the enjoyment of all that happiness which affluence and good breeding procure, and returned towards home, despairing of ever finding my daughter more, but sending a sigh to Heaven to spare and to forgive her.

I was now come within about twenty miles of home, having

hired a horse to carry me, as I was yet but weak, and comforted myself with the hopes of soon seeing all I held dearest upon earth. But the night coming on, I put up at a little public-house by the road-side, and asked for the landlord's company over a pint of wine. We sat beside his kitchen fire, which was the best room in the house, and chatted on politics and the news of the country. We happened, among other topics, to talk of young 'Squire Thornhill, who, the host assured me, was hated as much as his uncle Sir William, who sometimes came down to the country, was loved. He went on to observe, that he made it his whole study to betray the daughters of such as received him to their houses, and, after a fortnight or three weeks' possession, turned them out unrewarded, and abandoned to the world. As we continued our discourse in this manner, his wife, who had been out to get change, returned, and perceiving that her husband was enjoying a pleasure in which she was not a sharer, she asked him in angry tone, what he did there? to which he only replied, in an ironical way, by drinking her health. "Mr Symmonds," cried she, "you use me very ill, and I'll bear it no longer. Here three parts of the business is left for me to do, and the fourth left unfinished, while you do nothing but soak with the guests all day long; whereas, if a spoonful of liquor were to cure me of a fever, I never touch a drop." I now found what she would be at, and immediately poured her out a glass, which she received with a courtsey; and, drinking towards my good health, "Sir," resumed she, "it is not so much for the value of the liquor I am angry, but one cannot help it when the house is going out of the windows. If the customers or guests are to be dunned, all the burden lies upon my back; he'd as lief eat that glass as budge after them himself. There, now, above stairs, we have a young woman who has come to take up her lodging here, and I don't believe she has got any money, by her over-civility. I am certain she is very slow of payment, and I wish she were put in mind of it."—"What signifies minding her?" cried the host; "if she be slow she is sure."—"I don't know that," replied the wife; "but I know that I am sure she has been here a fortnight, and we have not yet seen the cross of her money."—"I suppose, my dear," cried he, "we shall have it all in a lump."—"In a lump!" cried the other; "I hope we may get it any way; and that I am resolved we will this very night, or out she tramps, bag and baggage."— "Consider, my dear," cried the husband, "she is a gentlewoman, and deserves more respect."—"As for the matter of that," re-turned the hostess, "gentle or simple, out she shall pack with a sussarara. Gentry may be good things where they take; but, for my part, I never saw much good of them at the sign of the Harrow." Thus saying, she ran up a narrow flight of stairs that went from the kitchen to a room overhead; and I soon per-ceived, by the loudness of her voice, and the bitterness of her reproaches, that no money was to be had from her lodger. I could hear her remonstrances very distinctly: "Out, I say; pack out this moment! tramp, thou infamous strumpet, or I'll give thee a mark thou won't be the better for this three months. What! you trumpery, to come and take up an honest house with-out cross or coin to bless yourself with! Come along, I say!"— "Oh, dear madam," cried the stranger, "pity me—pity a poor abandoned creature, for one night, and death will soon do the rest!" I instantly knew the voice of my poor ruined child Olivia. I flew to her rescue, while the woman was dragging her along by her hair, and I caught the dear forlorn wretch in my arms. "Welcome, any way welcome, my dearest lost one—my treasure —to your poor old father's bosom! Though the vicious forsake thee, there is yet one in the world that will never forsake thee; though thou hadst ten thousand crimes to answer for, he will forget them all!"—"Oh, my own dear,"—for minutes she could say no more—"my own dearest papa! Could angels be kinder? How do I deserve so much? The villain, I hate him and myself, to be a reproach to so much goodness! You can't forgive me, I know you cannot."—"Yes, my child, from my heart I do forgive thee: only repent, and we both shall yet be happy. We shall see many pleasant days yet, my Olivia."—"Ah! never, sir, never. The rest of my wretched life must be infamy abroad, and shame at home. But, alas! papa, you look much paler than you used to do. Could such a thing as I am give you so much uneasiness? Surely you have too much wisdom to take the miseries of my guilt upon yourself."—"Our wisdom, young woman," replied I. —"Ah, why so cold a name, papa?" cried she. "This is the first time you ever called me by so cold a name."—"I ask pardon, my darling," returned I; "but I was going to observe, that wisdom makes but a slow defence against trouble, though at last a sure one." The landlady now returned, to know if we did not choose a more genteel apartment; to which assenting, we were shown a room where we could converse more freely. After we had talked ourselves into some degree of tranquillity, I could not avoid desiring some account of the gradations that led her to her present wretched situation. "That villain, sir," said she, "from the first day of our meeting, made me honourable, though private proposals."

"Villain, indeed!" cried I; "and yet it in some measure surprises me how a person of Mr Burchell's good sense and seeming honour could be guilty of such deliberate baseness, and thus step into a family to undo it."

"My dear papa," returned my daughter, "you labour under a strange mistake. Mr Burchell never attempted to deceive me; instead of that, he took every opportunity of privately admonishing me against the artifices of Mr Thornhill, who, I now find, was even worse than he represented him."—"Mr Thornhill," in-

OLIVIA AND SQUIRE THORNHILL

terrupted I; "can it be?"—"Yes, Sir," returned she, "it was Mr Thornhill who seduced me; who employed the two ladies as he called them, but who in fact were abandoned women of the town, without breeding or pity, to decoy us up to London. Their artifices, you may remember, would have certainly succeeded but for Mr Burchell's letter, who directed those reproaches at them which we all applied to ourselves. How he came to have so much influence as to defeat their intentions still remains a secret to me; but I am convinced he was ever our warmest, sincerest friend."

"You amaze me, my dear," cried I; "but now I find my first suspicions of Mr Thornhill's baseness were too well grounded. But he can triumph in security; for he is rich, and we are poor. But tell me, my child, sure it was no small temptation that could thus obliterate all the impressions of such an education and so virtuous a disposition as thine?"

"Indeed, Sir," replied she, "he owes all his triumph to the desire I had of making him, and not myself, happy. I knew that the ceremony of our marriage, which was privately performed by a popish priest, was in no way binding, and that I had nothing to trust to but his honour."—"What!" interrupted I, "and were you indeed married by a priest in orders?"—"Indeed, Sir, we were," replied she, "though we were both sworn to conceal his name."—"Why, then, my child, come to my arms again; and now you are a thousand times more welcome than before; for you are now his wife to all intents and purposes; nor can all the laws of man, though written upon tables of adamant, lessen the force of that sacred connection."

"Alas! papa," replied she, "you are but little acquainted with his villainies. He has been married already by the same priest to six or eight wives more, whom, like me, he has deceived and abandoned."

131

"Has he so?" cried I, "then we must hang the priest, and you shall inform against him to-morrow."—"But, Sir," returned she, "will that be right, when I am sworn to secrecy?"—"My dear," I replied, "if you have made such a promise, I cannot, nor will I attempt you to break it. Even though it may benefit the public, you must not inform against him. In all human institutions a smaller evil is allowed to procure a greater good; as, in politics, a province may be given away to secure a kingdom; in medicine, a limb may be lopped off to preserve the body; but in religion the law is written, and inflexible, *never* to do evil. And this law, my child, is right; for otherwise, if we commit a smaller evil to procure a greater good, certain guilt would be thus incurred in expectation of contingent advantage. And though the advantage should certainly follow, yet the interval between commission and advantage, which is allowed to be guilty, may be that in which we are called away to answer for the things we have done, and the volume of human actions is closed for ever. But I interrupt you, my dear; go on."

"The very next morning," continued she, "I found what little expectation I was to have from his sincerity. That very morning he introduced me to two unhappy women more, whom, like me, he had deceived, but who lived in contented prostitution. I loved him too tenderly to bear such rivals in his affections, and strove to forget my infamy in a tumult of pleasures. With this view I danced, dressed, and talked; but still was unhappy. The gentlemen who visited there told me every moment of the power of my charms, and this only contributed to increase my melancholy, as I had thrown all their power quite away. Thus each day I grew more pensive, and he more insolent, till at last the monster had the assurance to offer me to a young baronet of his acquaintance. Need I describe, Sir, how his ingratitude stung me? My answer to this proposal was almost madness. I desired

132

to part. As I was going he offered me a purse: but I flung it at him with indignation, and burst from him in a rage, that for a while kept me insensible of the miseries of my situation. But I soon looked round me, and saw myself a vile, abject, guilty thing, without one friend in the world to apply to. Just in that interval, a stage coach happening to pass by, I took a place, it being my only aim to be driven at a distance from a wretch I despised and detested. I was set down here, where, since my arrival, my own anxiety and this woman's unkindness have been my only companions. The hours of pleasure that I have passed with my mamma and sister now grow painful to me. Their sorrows are much; but mine are greater than theirs, for mine are mixed with guilt and infamy."

"Have patience, my child," cried I, "and I hope things will yet be better. Take some repose to-night, and to-morrow I will carry you home to your mother and the rest of the family, from whom you will receive a kind reception. Poor woman! this has gone to her heart; but she loves you still, Olivia, and will forget it."

CHAPTER XXII

THE next morning I took my daughter behind me, and set out on my return home. As we travelled along I strove, by every persuasion, to calm her sorrows and fears, and to arm her with resolution to bear the presence of her offended mother. I took every opportunity, from the prospect of a fine country, through which we passed, to observe how much kinder Heaven was to us than we to each other; and that the misfortunes of Nature's making were very few. I assured her, that she should never perceive any change in my affections, and that, during my life, which yet might be long, she might depend upon a guardian and an instructor. I armed her against the censure of the world, showed her that books were sweet unreproaching companions to the miserable, and that, if they could not bring us to enjoy life, they would at least teach us to endure it.

The hired horse that we rode was to be put up that night at an inn by the way, within about five miles from my house; and as I was willing to prepare my family for my daughter's reception, I determined to leave her that night at the inn, and to re-

turn for her, accompanied by my daughter Sophia, early the
next morning. It was night before we reached our appointed
stage; however, after seeing her provided with a decent apartment, and having ordered the hostess to prepare proper refreshments, I kissed her, and proceeded towards home. And now
my heart caught new sensations of pleasure, the nearer I approached that peaceful mansion. As a bird that had been frightened from its nest, my affections outwent my haste, and hovered
round my little fireside with all the rapture of expectation. I
called up the many fond things I had to say, and anticipated
the welcome I was to receive. I already felt my wife's tender
embrace, and smiled at the joy of my little ones. As I walked
but slowly, the night waned apace. The labourers of the day
were all retired to rest; the lights were out in every cottage; no
sounds were heard but of the shrilling cock, and the deep-
mouthed watch-dog, at hollow distance. I approached my little
abode of pleasure, and, before I was within a furlong of the
place, our honest mastiff came running to welcome me.

It was now near midnight that I came to knock at my door;
all was still and silent; my heart dilated with unutterable happiness, when, to my amazement, I saw the house bursting out in
a blaze of fire, and every aperture red with conflagration. I gave
a loud convulsive outcry, and fell upon the pavement, insensible. This alarmed my son, who had, till this, been asleep; and
he, perceiving the flames, instantly waked my wife and daughter; and all running out, naked, and wild with apprehension,
recalled me to life with their anguish. But it was only to objects
of new terror; for the flames had, by this time, caught the roof
of our dwelling, part after part continuing to fall in, while the
family stood, with silent agony, looking on, as if they enjoyed
the blaze. I gazed upon them and upon it by turns, and then
looked round me for my two little ones; but they were not to be

135

seen. O misery! "Where," cried I, "where are my little ones?"—
"They are burnt to death in the flames," said my wife calmly,
"and I will die with them." That moment I heard the cry of the
babes within, who were just awaked by the fire, and nothing
could have stopped me. "Where, where are my children?" cried
I, rushing through the flames, and bursting the door of the
chamber in which they were confined!—"Where are my little
ones?"—"Here, dear papa, here we are," cried they together,
while the flames were just catching the bed where they lay. I
caught them both in my arms, and snatched them through the
fire as fast as possible, while, just as I got out, the roof sunk in.
"Now," cried I, holding up my children, "now let the flames
burn on, and all my possessions perish. Here they are; I have
saved my treasure. Here, my dearest, here are our treasures,
and we shall yet be happy." We kissed our little darlings a thousand times; they clasped us round the neck, and seemed to share
our transports, while their mother laughed and wept by turns.

I now stood a calm spectator of the flames; and, after some
time, began to perceive that my arm to the shoulder was
scorched in a terrible manner. It was, therefore, out of my
power to give my son any assistance, either in attempting to
save our goods, or preventing the flames spreading to our corn.
By this time the neighbours were alarmed, and came running
to our assistance; but all they could do was to stand, like us—
spectators of the calamity.

My goods, among which were the notes I had reserved for
my daughters' fortunes, were entirely consumed, except a box
with some papers that stood in the kitchen, and two or three
things more of little consequence, which my son brought away
in the beginning. The neighbours contributed, however, what
they could to lighten our distress. They brought us clothes, and
furnished one of our outhouses with kitchen utensils; so that by

daylight we had another, though a wretched dwelling, to retire to. My honest next neighbour and his children were not the least assiduous in providing us with everything necessary, and offering whatever consolation untutored benevolence could suggest.

When the fears of my family had subsided, curiosity to know the cause of my long stay began to take place: having therefore informed them of every particular, I proceeded to prepare them for the reception of our lost one; and though we had nothing but wretchedness now to impart, I was willing to procure her a welcome to what we had. This task would have been more difficult but for our recent calamity, which had humbled my wife's pride, and blunted it by more poignant afflictions. Being unable to go for my poor child myself, as my arm grew very painful, I sent my son and daughter, who soon returned, supporting the wretched delinquent, who had not the courage to look up at her mother, whom no instructions of mine could persuade to a perfect reconciliation; for women have a much stronger sense of female error than men. "Ah, madam," cried her mother, "this is but a poor place you are come to after so much finery. My daughter Sophy and I can afford but little entertainment to persons who have kept company only with people of distinction. Yes, Miss Livy, your poor father and I have suffered very much of late; but I hope Heaven will forgive you." During this reception, the unhappy victim stood pale and trembling, unable to weep or to reply: but I could not continue a silent spectator of her distress; wherefore, assuming a degree of severity in my voice and manner which was ever followed with instant submission, "I entreat, woman, that my words may be now marked once for all: I have here brought you back a poor deluded wanderer; her return to duty demands the revival of our tenderness. The real hardships of life are now coming fast upon us; let us not, therefore, increase them by dissension among each other. If we live harmoniously together, we may yet be contented, as there are enough of us to shut out the censuring world and keep each other in countenance. The kindness of Heaven is promised to the penitent, and let ours be directed by the example. Heaven, we are assured, is much more pleased to view a repentant sinner, than ninety-nine persons who have supported a course of undeviating rectitude. And this is right; for that single effort by which we stop short in the down-hill path to perdition, is itself a greater exertion of virtue than an hundred acts of justice."

CHAPTER XXIII

SOME assiduity was now required to make our present abode
as convenient as possible, and we were soon again qualified to
enjoy our former serenity. Being disabled myself from assisting
my son in our usual occupations, I read to my family from the
few books that were saved, and particularly from such as, by
amusing the imagination, contributed to ease the heart. Our
good neighbours, too, came every day with the kindest condo-
lence, and fixed a time in which they were all to assist at repair-
ing my former dwelling. Honest Farmer Williams was not last
among these visitors; but heartily offered his friendship. He
would even have renewed his addresses to my daughter; but
she rejected him in such a manner, as totally repressed his future solicitations. Her grief seemed formed for continuing; and
she was the only person of our little society that a week did not
restore to cheerfulness. She now lost that unblushing innocence
which once taught her to respect herself, and to seek pleasure
by pleasing. Anxiety now had taken strong possession of her
mind; her beauty began to be impaired with her constitution,

and neglect still more contributed to diminish it. Every tender epithet bestowed on her sister brought a pang to her heart, and a tear to her eye; and as one vice, though cured, ever plants others where it has been, so her former guilt, though driven out by repentance, left jealousy and envy behind. I strove a thousand ways to lessen her care, and even forgot my own pain in a concern for hers, collecting such amusing passages of history as a strong memory and some reading could suggest. "Our happiness, my dear," I would say, "is in the power of One who can bring it about in a thousand unforeseen ways, that mock our foresight. If example be necessary to prove this, I'll give you a story, my child, told us by a grave, though sometimes a romancing historian.

"Matilda was married very young to a Neapolitan nobleman of the first quality, and found herself a widow and a mother at the age of fifteen. As she stood one day caressing her infant son in the open window of an apartment which hung over the river Volturna, the child with a sudden spring leaped from her arms into the flood below, and disappeared in a moment. The mother, struck with instant surprise, and making an effort to save him, plunged in after; but far from being able to assist the infant, she herself with great difficulty escaped to the opposite shore, just when some French soldiers were plundering the country on that side, who immediately made her their prisoner.

"As the war was then carried on between the French and Italians with the utmost inhumanity, they were going at once to perpetrate those two extremes suggested by appetite and cruelty. This base resolution, however, was opposed by a young officer, who, though their retreat required the utmost expedition, placed her behind him, and brought her in safety to his native city. Her beauty at first caught his eye; her merit, soon after, his heart. They were married; he rose to the highest posts;

140

they lived long together, and were happy. But the felicity of a soldier can never be called permanent; after an interval of several years, the troops which he commanded having met with a repulse, he was obliged to take shelter in the city where he had lived with his wife. Here they suffered a siege, and the city at length was taken. Few histories can produce more various instances of cruelty than those which the French and Italians at that time exercised upon each other. It was resolved by the victors, upon this occasion, to put all the French prisoners to death; but particularly the husband of the unfortunate Matilda, as he was principally instrumental in protracting the siege. Their determinations were, in general, executed almost as soon as resolved upon. The captive soldier was led forth, and the executioner with his sword stood ready, while the spectators in gloomy silence awaited the fatal blow, which was only suspended till the general who presided as judge should give the signal. It was in this interval of anguish and expectation that Matilda came to take her last farewell of her husband and deliverer, deploring her wretched situation, and the cruelty of fate, that had saved her from perishing by a premature death in the river Volturna, to be the spectator of still greater calamities. The general, who was a young man, was struck with surprise at her beauty, and pity at her distress; but with still stronger emotions when he heard her mention her former dangers. He was her son, the infant for whom she had encountered so much danger. He acknowledged her at once as his mother, and fell at her feet. The rest may be easily supposed; the captive was set free, and all the happiness that love, friendship, and duty could confer on each, were united."

In this manner I would attempt to amuse my daughter: but she listened with divided attention; for her own misfortunes engrossed all the pity she once had for those of another, and nothing gave her ease. In company she dreaded contempt; and in solitude she only found anxiety. Such was the colour of her wretchedness, when we received certain information that Mr Thornhill was going to be married to Miss Wilmot, for whom I always suspected he had a real passion, though he took every opportunity before me to express his contempt both of her person and fortune. This news only served to increase poor Olivia's affliction: such a flagrant breach of fidelity was more than her courage could support. I was resolved, however, to get more certain information, and to defeat, if possible, the completion of his designs, by sending my son to old Mr Wilmot's with instructions to know the truth of the report, and to deliver Miss Wilmot a letter, intimating Mr Thornhill's conduct in my family. My son went in pursuance of my directions, and in three days returned, assuring us of the truth of the account; but that he had found it impossible to deliver the letter, which he was therefore obliged to leave, as Mr Thornhill and Miss Wilmot were visiting round the country. They were to be married, he said, in a few days, having appeared together at church the Sunday before he was there, in great splendour, the bride attended by six young ladies, and he by as many gentlemen. Their approaching nuptials filled the whole country with rejoicing, and they usually rode out together in the grandest equipage that had been seen in the country for many years. All the friends of both families, he said, were there, particularly the 'Squire's uncle, Sir William Thornhill, who bore so good a character. He added, that nothing but mirth and feasting were going forward; that all the country praised the young bride's beauty, and the bridegroom's fine person, and that they were immensely fond of each other; concluding, that he could not help thinking Mr Thornhill one of the most happy men in the world.

"Why, let him, if he can," returned I: "but, my son, observe this bed of straw and unsheltering roof; those mouldering walls and humid floor; my wretched body thus disabled by fire, and my children weeping round me for bread: you have come home, my child, to all this; yet here, even here, you see a man that would not for a thousand worlds exchange situations. Oh, my children, if you could but learn to commune with your own hearts, and know what noble company you can make them, you would little regard the elegance and splendour of the worthless. Almost all men have been taught to call life a passage, and themselves the travellers. The similitude still may be improved, when we observe that the good are joyful and serene, like travellers that are going towards home; the wicked but by intervals happy, like travellers that are going into exile."

My compassion for my poor daughter, overpowered by this new disaster, interrupted what I had further to observe. I bade her mother support her, and after a short time she recovered. She appeared from that time more calm, and I imagined had gained a new degree of resolution; but appearances deceived me: for her tranquillity was the languor of overwrought resentment. A supply of provisions, charitably sent us by my kind parishioners, seemed to diffuse new cheerfulness among the rest of the family, nor was I displeased at seeing them once more sprightly and at ease. It would have been unjust to damp their satisfactions, merely to condole with resolute melancholy, or to burden them with a sadness they did not feel. Thus once more the tale went round, and the song was demanded, and cheerfulness condescended to hover round our little habitation.

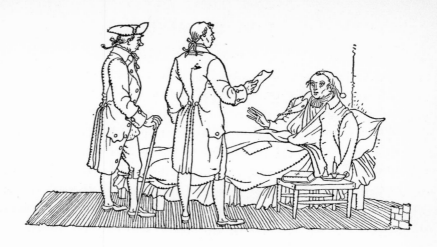

CHAPTER XXIV

THE next morning the sun arose with peculiar warmth for the season, so that we agreed to breakfast together on the honeysuckle bank; where, while we sat, my youngest daughter at my request joined her voice to the concert on the trees above us. It was in this place my poor Olivia first met her seducer, and every object served to recall her sadness. But that melancholy which is excited by objects of pleasure, or inspired by sounds of harmony, soothes the heart instead of corroding it. Her mother, too, upon this occasion, felt a pleasing distress, and wept, and loved her daughter as before. "Do, my pretty Olivia," cried she, "let us have that little melancholy air your papa was so fond of; your sister Sophy has already obliged us. Do, child; it will please your old father." She complied in a manner so exquisitely pathetic as moved me:

> When lovely woman stoops to folly,
>   And finds too late that men betray,
> What charm can soothe her melancholy?
>   What art can wash her guilt away?

The only art her guilt to cover,
  To hide her shame from every eye,
To give repentance to her lover,
  And wring his bosom, is—to die.

As she was concluding the last stanza, to which an interruption in her voice from sorrow gave peculiar softness, the appearance of Mr Thornhill's equipage at a distance alarmed us all, but particularly increased the uneasiness of my eldest daughter, who, desirous of shunning her betrayer, returned to the house with her sister. In a few minutes he was alighted from his chariot, and making up to the place where I was still sitting, inquired after my health with his usual air of familiarity. "Sir," replied I, "your present assurance only serves to aggravate the baseness of your character; and there was a time when I would have chastised your insolence for presuming thus to appear before me. But now you are safe; for age has cooled my passions, and my calling restrains them."

"I vow, my dear Sir," returned he, "I am amazed at all this; nor can I understand what it means! I hope you don't think your daughter's late excursion with me had anything criminal in it?"

"Go," cried I, "thou art a wretch, a poor, pitiful wretch, and every way a liar: but your meanness secures you from my anger! Yet, Sir, I am descended from a family that would not have borne this!—And so, thou vile thing, to gratify a momentary passion, thou hast made one poor creature wretched for life, and polluted a family that had nothing but honour for their portion!"

"If she or you," returned he, "are resolved to be miserable, I cannot help it. But you may still be happy; and whatever opinion you may have formed of me, you shall ever find me ready to contribute to it. We can marry her to another in a short time;

and what is more, she may keep her lover beside; for I protest I shall ever continue to have a true regard for her."

I found all my passions alarmed at this new degrading proposal; for though the mind may often be calm under great injuries, little villainy can at any time get within the soul, and sting it into rage.—"Avoid my sight, thou reptile!" cried I, "nor continue to insult me with thy presence. Were my brave son at home, he would not suffer this; but I am old and disabled, and every way undone."

"I find," cried he, "you are bent upon obliging me to talk in a harsher manner than I intended. But as I have shown you what may be hoped from my friendship, it may not be improper to represent what may be the consequences of my resentment. My attorney, to whom your late bond has been transferred, threatens hard; nor do I know how to prevent the course of justice, except by paying the money myself, which, as I have been at some expenses lately previous to my intended marriage, is not so easy to be done. And then my steward talks of driving for the rent; it is certain he knows his duty; for I never trouble myself with affairs of that nature. Yet still I could wish to serve you, and even to have you and your daughter present at my marriage, which is shortly to be solemnized with Miss Wilmot; it is even the request of my charming Arabella herself, whom I hope you will not refuse."

"Mr Thornhill," replied I, "hear me once for all: as to your marriage with any but my daughter, that I never will consent to; and though your friendship could raise me to a throne, or your resentment sink me to the grave yet would I despise both. Thou hast once woefully, irreparably deceived me. I reposed my heart upon thine honour, and have found its baseness. Never more, therefore, expect friendship from me. Go, and possess what fortune has given thee—beauty, riches, health, and pleasure. Go, and leave me to want, infamy, disease, and sorrow. Yet, humbled as I am, shall my heart still vindicate its dignity; and though thou hast my forgiveness, thou shalt ever have my contempt."

"If so," returned he, "depend upon it you shall feel the effects of this insolence; and we shall shortly see which is the fittest object of scorn, you or me."—Upon which he departed abruptly.

My wife and son, who were present at this interview, seemed terrified with apprehension. My daughters also, finding that he was gone, came out to be informed of the result of our conference, which, when known, alarmed them not less than the rest. But as to myself, I disregarded the utmost stretch of his malevolence: he had already struck the blow, and now I stood prepared to repel every new effort, like one of those instruments used in the art of war, which, however thrown, still presents a point to receive the enemy.

We soon, however, found that he had not threatened in vain; for the very next morning his steward came to demand my annual rent, which, by the train of accidents already related, I was unable to pay. The consequence of my incapacity was his driving my cattle that evening, and their being appraised and sold the next day for less than half their value. My wife and children now therefore entreated me to comply upon any terms, rather than incur certain destruction. They even begged of me to admit his visits once more, and used all their little eloquence to paint the calamities I was going to endure,—the terrors of a prison in so rigorous a season as the present, with the danger that threatened my health from the late accident that happened by the fire. But I continued inflexible.

"Why, my treasures," cried I, "why will you thus attempt to persuade me to the thing that is not right? My duty has taught

147

me to forgive him; but my conscience will not permit me to approve. Would you have me applaud to the world what my heart must internally condemn? Would you have me tamely sit down and flatter our infamous betrayer; and, to avoid a prison, continually suffer the more galling bonds of mental confinement? No, never! If we are to be taken from this abode, only let us hold to the right; and wherever we are thrown, we can still retire to a charming apartment, when we can look round our own hearts with intrepidity and with pleasure!"

In this manner we spent that evening. Early the next morning, as the snow had fallen in great abundance in the night, my son was employed in clearing it away, and opening a passage before the door. He had not been thus engaged long, when he came running in, with looks all pale, to tell us that two strangers, whom he knew to be officers of justice, were making towards the house.

Just as he spoke they came in, and approaching the bed where I lay, after previously informing me of their employment and business, made me their prisoner, bidding me prepare to go with them to the county gaol, which was eleven miles off.

"My friends," said I, "this is severe weather in which you have come to take me to a prison; and it is particularly unfortunate at this time, as one of my arms has lately been burnt in a terrible manner, and it has thrown me into a slight fever, and I want clothes to cover me, and I am now too weak and old to walk far in such deep snow; but, if it must be so——"

I then turned to my wife and children, and directed them to get together what few things were left us, and to prepare immediately for leaving this place. I entreated them to be expeditious; and desired my son to assist his eldest sister, who, from a consciousness that she was the cause of all our calamities, was fallen, and had lost anguish in insensibility. I encouraged my

148

wife, who, pale and trembling, clasped our affrighted little ones in her arms, that clung to her bosom in silence, dreading to look round at the strangers. In the meantime my youngest daughter prepared for our departure, and as she received several hints to use despatch, in about an hour we were ready to depart.

CHAPTER XXV

W<small>E</small> set forward from this peaceful neighbourhood and walked on slowly. My eldest daughter being enfeebled by a slow fever, which had begun for some days to undermine her constitution, one of the officers who had an horse kindly took her behind him; for even these men cannot entirely divest themselves of humanity. My son led one of the little ones by the hand, and my wife the other, while I leaned upon my youngest girl, whose tears fell, not for her own, but my distresses.

We were now got from my late dwelling about two miles, when we saw a crowd running and shouting behind us, consisting of about fifty of my poorest parishioners. These, with dreadful imprecations, soon seized upon the two officers of justice, and swearing they would never see their minister go to gaol while they had a drop of blood to shed in his defence, were going to use them with great severity. The consequence might have been fatal, had I not immediately interposed, and with some difficulty rescued the officers from the hands of the en-

150

raged multitude. My children, who looked upon my delivery now as certain, appeared transported with joy, and were incapable of containing their raptures. But they were soon undeceived, upon hearing me address the poor deluded people, who came, as they imagined, to do me service.

"What! my friends," cried I, "and is this the way you love me? Is this the manner you obey the instructions I have given you from the pulpit? Thus to fly in the face of justice, and bring down ruin on yourselves and me? Which is your ringleader? Show me the man that has thus seduced you. As sure as he lives he shall feel my resentment. Alas! my dear deluded flock, return back to the duty you owe to God, to your country and to me. I shall yet perhaps one day see you in greater felicity here, and contribute to make your lives more happy. But, let it at least be my comfort, when I pen my fold for immortality, that not one here shall be wanting."

They now seemed all repentance, and melting into tears, came one after the other to bid me farewell. I shook each tenderly by the hand, and leaving them my blessing, proceeded forward without meeting any further interruption. Some hours before night, we reached the town, or rather village, for it consisted but of a few mean houses, having lost all its former opulence, and retaining no marks of its ancient superiority but the gaol.

Upon entering we put up at an inn, where we had such refreshments as could most readily be procured, and I supped with my family with my usual cheerfulness. After seeing them properly accommodated for that night, I next attended the sheriff's officers to the prison, which had formerly been built for the purposes of war, and consisted of one large apartment, strongly grated, and paved with stone, common to both felons and debtors at certain hours in the four-and-twenty. Besides this, every prisoner had a separate cell, where he was locked in for the night.

I expected, upon my entrance, to find nothing but lamentations and various sounds of misery: but it was very different. The prisoners seemed all employed in one common design, that of forgetting thought in merriment or clamour. I was apprised of the usual perquisites required upon these occasions, and immediately complied with the demand, though the little money I had was very near being all exhausted. This was immediately sent away for liquor, and the whole prison was soon filled with riot, laughter, and profaneness.

"How," cried I to myself, "shall men so very wicked be cheerful, and shall I be melancholy? I feel only the same confinement with them, and I think I have more reason to be happy."

With such reflections I laboured to become cheerful; but cheerfulness was never yet produced by effort, which is itself painful. As I was sitting, therefore, in a corner of the gaol, in a pensive posture, one of my fellow-prisoners came up, and, sitting by me, entered into conversation. It was my constant rule in life never to avoid the conversation of any man who seemed to desire it; for if good, I might profit by his instruction; if bad, he might be assisted by mine. I found this to be a knowing man, of strong unlettered sense, but a thorough knowledge of the world, as it is called, or more properly speaking, of human nature on the wrong side. He asked me if I had taken care to provide myself with a bed, which was a circumstance I had never once attended to.

"That's unfortunate," cried he, "as you are allowed here nothing but straw, and your apartment is very large and cold. However, you seem to be something of a gentleman, and, as I have been one myself in my time, part of my bed-clothes are heartily at your service."

152

I thanked him, professing my surprise at finding such humanity in a gaol in misfortunes; adding, to let him see that I was a scholar, "That the sage ancient seemed to understand the value of company in affliction, when he said, *Ton kosmon aire, ei dos ton etairon;* and, in fact," continued I, "what is the world if it affords only solitude?"

"You talk of the world, Sir," returned my fellow-prisoner; "the world is in its dotage: and yet the cosmogony or creation of the world has puzzled the philosophers of every age. What a medley of opinions have they not broached upon the creation of the world! Sanchoniathon, Manetho, Berosus, and Ocellus Lucanus, have all attempted it in vain. The latter has these words, *Anarchon ara kai atelutaion to pan,* which implies——" "I ask pardon, Sir," cried I, "for interrupting so much learning: but I think I have heard all this before. Have I not had the pleasure of once seeing you at Wellbridge fair, and is not your name Ephraim Jenkinson?" At this demand he only sighed. "I suppose you must recollect," resumed I, "one Doctor Primrose, from whom you bought a horse?"

He now at once recollected me; for the gloominess of the place and the approaching night had prevented his distinguishing my features before. "Yes, Sir," returned Mr Jenkinson, "I remember you perfectly well; I bought a horse, but forgot to pay for him. Your neighbour Flamborough is the only prosecutor I am any way afraid of at the next assizes; for he intends to swear positively against me as a coiner. I am heartily sorry, Sir, I ever deceived you, or indeed any man; for you see," continued he, showing his shackles, "what my tricks have brought me to."

"Well, Sir," replied I, "your kindness in offering me assistance when you could expect no return, shall be repaid with my endeavours to soften, or totally suppress Mr Flamborough's evidence, and I will send my son to him for that purpose the first opportunity; nor do I in the least doubt but he will comply with my request; and as to my own evidence, you need be under no uneasiness about that."

"Well, Sir," cried he, "all the return I can make shall be yours. You shall have more than half my bed-clothes to-night, and I'll take care to stand your friend in the prison, where I think I have some influence."

I thanked him, and could not avoid being surprised at the present youthful change in his aspect; for at the time I had seen him before, he appeared at least sixty. "Sir," answered he, "you are little acquainted with the world; I had at that time, false hair, and have learnt the art of counterfeiting every age from seventeen to seventy. Ah, Sir! had I but bestowed half the pains in learning a trade that I have in learning to be a scoundrel, I might have been a rich man at this day. But, rogue as I am, still I may be your friend, and that, perhaps, when you least expect it."

We were now prevented from further conversation by the arrival of the gaoler's servants, who came to call over the prisoners' names, and lock up for the night. A fellow also, with a bundle of straw for my bed, attended, who led me along a dark narrow passage, into a room paved like the common prison, and in one corner of this I spread my bed, and the clothes given me by my fellow-prisoner; which done, my conductor, who was civil enough, bade me a good night. After my usual meditations, and having praised my heavenly corrector, I laid myself down, and slept with the utmost tranquillity till morning.

CHAPTER XXVI

THE next morning early I was awakened by my family, whom I found in tears at my bedside. The gloomy strength of everything about us, it seems, had daunted them. I gently rebuked their sorrow, assuring them I had never slept with greater tranquillity; and next inquired after my eldest daughter, who was not among them. They informed me that yesterday's uneasiness and fatigue had increased her fever, and it was judged proper to leave her behind. My next care was to send my son to procure a room or two to lodge the family in, as near the prison as conveniently could be found. He obeyed; but could only find one apartment, which was hired at a small expense for his mother and sisters, the gaoler, with humanity, consenting to let him and his two little brothers lie in the prison with me. A bed was therefore prepared for them in a corner of the room, which I thought answered very conveniently. I was willing, however, previously to know whether my little children chose to lie in a place which seemed to fright them upon entrance.

"Well," cried I, "my good boys, how do you like your bed?

155

I hope you are not afraid to lie in this room, dark as it appears?"

"No, papa," says Dick, "I am not afraid to lie anywhere, where you are."

"And I," says Bill, who was yet but four years old, "love every place best that my papa is in."

After this I allotted to each of the family what they were to do. My daughter was particularly directed to watch her declining sister's health; my wife was to attend me; my little boys were to read to me: "And as for you, my son," continued I, "it is by the labour of your hands we must all hope to be supported. Your wages as a day-labourer will be fully sufficient, with proper frugality, to maintain us all, and comfortably too. Thou art now sixteen years old, and hast strength; and it was given thee, my son, for very useful purposes; for it must save from famine your helpless parents and family. Prepare then, this evening, to look out for work against to-morrow, and bring home every night what money you earn for our support."

Having thus instructed him, and settled the rest, I walked down to the common prison, where I could enjoy more air and room. But I was not long there when the execrations, lewdness, and brutality that invaded me on every side, drove me back to my apartment again. Here I sat for some time pondering upon the strange infatuation of wretches, who, finding all mankind in open arms against them, were labouring to make themselves a future and a tremendous enemy.

Their insensibility excited my highest compassion, and blotted my own uneasiness from my mind. It even appeared a duty incumbent upon me to attempt to reclaim them. I resolved, therefore, once more to return, and, in spite of their contempt, to give them my advice, and conquer them by my perseverance. Going, therefore, among them again, I informed Mr Jenkinson of my design, at which he laughed heartily, but communicated

THE VICAR IN PRISON

it to the rest. The proposal was received with the greatest good humour, as it promised to afford a new fund of entertainment to persons who had now no other resource for mirth but what could be derived from ridicule or debauchery.

I therefore read them a portion of the service with a loud, unaffected voice, and found my audience perfectly merry upon the occasion. Lewd whispers, groans of contrition burlesqued, winking and coughing, alternately excited laughter. However, I continued with my natural solemnity to read on, sensible that what I did might mend some, but could itself receive no contamination from any.

After reading, I entered upon my exhortation, which was rather calculated at first to amuse them than to reprove. I previously observed, that no other motive but their welfare could induce me to this; that I was their fellow-prisoner, and now got nothing by preaching. I was sorry, I said, to hear them so very profane; because they got nothing by it, but might lose a great deal: "For be assured, my friends," cried I,—"for you are my friends, however the world may disclaim your friendship,— though you swore twelve thousand oaths in a day, it would not put one penny in your purse. Then what signifies calling every moment upon the devil, and courting his friendship, since you find how scurvily he uses you? He has given you nothing here, you find, but a mouthful of oaths and an empty belly; and, by the best accounts I have of him, he will give you nothing that's good hereafter.

"If used ill in our dealings with one man, we naturally go elsewhere. Were it not worth your while, then, just to try how you may like the usage of another master, who gives you fair promises at least to come to him? Surely, my friends, of all stupidity in the world, his must be the greatest, who, after robbing a house, runs to the thief-takers for protection. And yet,

157

how are you more wise? You are all seeking comfort from one that has already betrayed you, applying to a more malicious being than any thief-taker of them all; for they only decoy and then hang you; but he decoys and hangs, and, what is worst of all, will not let you loose after the hangman has done."

When I had concluded, I received the compliments of my audience, some of whom came and shook me by the hand, swearing that I was a very honest fellow, and that they desired my further acquaintance. I therefore promised to repeat my lecture next day, and actually conceived some hopes of making a reformation here; for it had ever been my opinion, that no man was past the hour of amendment, every heart lying open to the shafts of reproof; if the archer could but take a proper aim. When I had thus satisfied my mind, I went back to my apartment, where my wife prepared a frugal meal, while Mr Jenkinson begged leave to add his dinner to ours, and partake of the pleasure, as he was kind enough to express it, of my conversation. He had not yet seen my family; for as they came to my apartment by a door in the narrow passage already described, by this means they avoided the common prison. Jenkinson at the first interview, therefore, seemed not a little struck with the beauty of my youngest daughter, which her pensive air contributed to heighten; and my little ones did not pass unnoticed.

"Alas, Doctor," cried he, "these children are too handsome and too good for such a place as this!"

"Why, Mr Jenkinson," replied I, "thank Heaven, my children are pretty tolerable in morals; and if they be good, it matters little for the rest."

"I fancy, Sir," returned my fellow-prisoner, "that it must give you great comfort to have all this little family about you."

"A comfort, Mr Jenkinson!" replied I; "yes, it is indeed a comfort, and I would not be without them for all the world; for they can make a dungeon seem a palace. There is but one way in this life of wounding my happiness, and that is by injuring them."

"I am afraid then, Sir," cried he, "that I am in some measure culpable; for I think I see here (looking at my son Moses) one that I have injured, and by whom I wish to be forgiven."

My son immediately recollected his voice and features, though he had before seen him in disguise, and taking him by the hand, with a smile, forgave him. "Yet," continued he, "I can't help wondering at what you could see in my face, to think me a proper mark for deception."

"My dear Sir," returned the other, "it was not your face, but your white stockings, and the black ribbon in your hair, that allured me. But, no disparagement to your parts, I have deceived wiser men than you in my time; and yet, with all my tricks, the blockheads have been too many for me at last."

"I suppose," cried my son, "that the narrative of such a life as yours must be extremely instructive and amusing."

"Not much of either," returned Mr Jenkinson. "Those relations which describe the tricks and vices only of mankind, by increasing our suspicion in life, retard our success. The traveller that distrusts every person he meets, and turns back upon the appearance of every man that looks like a robber, seldom arrives in time at his journey's end.

"Indeed, I think, from my own experience, that the knowing one is the silliest fellow under the sun. I was thought cunning from my very childhood; when but seven years old, the ladies would say that I was a perfect little man; at fourteen, I knew the world, cocked my hat, and loved the ladies; at twenty, though I was perfectly honest, yet every one thought me so cunning, that no one would trust me. Thus I was at last obliged to turn sharper in my own defence, and have lived ever since, my head throbbing with schemes to deceive, and my heart pal-

159

pitating with fears of detection. I used often to laugh at your honest simple neighbour Flamborough, and, one way or another, generally cheated him once a year. Yet still the honest man went forward without suspicion, and grew rich, while I still continued tricksy and cunning, and was poor, without the consolation of being honest. However," continued he, "let me know your case, and what has brought you here; perhaps, though I have not skill to avoid a gaol myself, I may extricate my friends."

In compliance with his curiosity, I informed him of the whole train of accidents and follies that had plunged me into my present troubles, and my utter inability to get free.

After hearing my story, and pausing some minutes, he slapped his forehead, as if he had hit upon something material, and took his leave, saying, he would try what could be done.

CHAPTER XXVII

THE next morning I communicated to my wife and children the scheme I had planned of reforming the prisoners, which they received with universal disapprobation, alleging the impossibility and impropriety of it; adding that my endeavours would no way contribute to their amendment, but might probably disgrace my calling.

"Excuse me," returned I; "these people, however fallen, are still men; and that is a very good title to my affections. Good counsel rejected returns to enrich the giver's bosom; and though the instruction I communicate may not mend them, yet it will assuredly mend myself. If these wretches, my children, were princes, there would be thousands ready to offer their ministry; but in my opinion, the heart that is buried in a dungeon is as precious as that seated upon a throne. Yes, my treasures, if I can mend them, I will: perhaps they will not all despise me. Perhaps I may catch up even one from the gulf, and that will be great gain; for is there upon earth a gem so precious as the human soul?"

Thus saying, I left them, and descended to the common prison, where I found the prisoners very merry expecting my arrival; and each prepared with some gaol trick to play upon the Doctor. Thus, as I was going to begin, one turned my wig awry, as if by accident, and then asked my pardon. A second, who stood at some distance, had a knack of spitting through his teeth, which fell in showers on my book. A third would cry Amen in such an affected tone as gave the rest great delight. A fourth had slyly picked my pocket of my spectacles. But there was one whose trick gave more universal pleasure than all the rest; for, observing the manner in which I had disposed my books on the table before me, he very dexterously displaced one of them, and put an obscene jest-book of his own in the place. However, I took no notice of all that this mischievous group of little beings could do, but went on, perfectly sensible that what was ridiculous in my attempt would excite mirth only the first or second time, while what was serious would be permanent. My design succeeded, and in less than six days some were penitent, and all attentive.

It was now that I applauded my perseverance and address, at thus giving sensibility to wretches divested of every moral feeling, and now began to think of doing them temporal services also, by rendering their situation somewhat more comfortable. Their time had hitherto been divided between famine and excess, tumultuous riot and bitter repining. Their only employment was quarrelling among each other, playing at cribbage, and cutting tobacco-stoppers. From this last mode of idle industry I took the hint of setting such as chose to work at cutting pegs for tobacconists and shoemakers, the proper wood being bought by a general subscription, and, when manufactured, sold by my appointment; so that each earned something every day—a trifle indeed, but sufficient to maintain him.

I did not stop here, but instituted fines for the punishment of immorality, and rewards for peculiar industry. Thus in less than a fortnight I had formed them into something social and humane, and had the pleasure of regarding myself as a legislator, who had brought men from their native ferocity into friendship and obedience.

And it were highly to be wished, that legislative power would thus direct the law rather to reformation than severity; that it would seem convinced that the work of eradicating crimes is not by making punishment familiar, but formidable. Then, instead of our present prisons, which find or make men guilty, which enclose wretches for the commission of one crime, and return them, if returned alive, fitted for the perpetration of thousands; we should see, as in other parts of Europe, places of penitence and solitude, where the accused might be attended by such as could give them repentance, if guilty, or new motives to virtue, if innocent. And this, but not the increasing punishments, is the way to mend a state. Nor can I avoid even questioning the validity of that right which social combinations have assumed, of capitally punishing offences of a slight nature. In cases of murder, their right is obvious, as it is the duty of us all, from the law of self-defence, to cut off that man who has shown a disregard for the life of another. Against such, all nature rises in arms; but it is not so against him who steals my property. Natural law gives me no right to take away his life, as, by that, the horse he steals is as much his property as mine. If, then, I have any right, it must be from a compact made between us, that he who deprives the other of his horse shall die. But this is a false compact; because no man has a right to barter his life no more than to take it away, as it is not his own. And besides, the compact is inadequate, and would be set aside, even in a court of modern equity, as there is a great penalty for a very trifling convenience, since it is far better that two men should live than that one man should ride. But a compact that is false between two men, is equally so between a hundred or a hundred thousand; for as ten millions of circles can never make a square, so the united voice of myriads cannot lend the smallest foundation to falsehood. It is thus that reason speaks, and untutored nature says the same thing. Savages, that are directed by natural law alone, are very tender of the lives of each other; they seldom shed blood but to retaliate former cruelty.

Our Saxon ancestors, fierce as they were in war, had but few executions in times of peace; and, in all commencing governments that have the print of nature still strong upon them, scarce any crime is held capital.

It is among the citizens of a refined community that penal laws, which are in the hands of the rich, are laid upon the poor. Government, while it grows older, seems to acquire the moroseness of age, and, as if our property were become dearer in proportion as it increased—as if the more enormous our wealth the more extensive our fears—all our possessions are paled up with new edicts every day, and hung round with gibbets to scare every invader.

I cannot tell whether it is from the number of our penal laws, or the licentiousness of our people, that this country should show more convicts in a year than half the dominions of Europe united. Perhaps it is owing to both; for they mutually produce each other. When, by indiscriminate penal laws, a nation beholds the same punishment affixed to dissimilar degrees of guilt, from perceiving no distinction in the penalty, the people are led to lose all sense of distinction in the crime, and this distinction is the bulwark of all morality; thus the multitude of laws produce new vices, and new vices call for fresh restraints.

It were to be wished, then, that power, instead of contriving new laws to punish vice; instead of drawing hard the cords of society till a convulsion come to burst them; instead of cutting away wretches as useless before we have tried their utility; instead of converting correction into vengeance,—it were to be wished that we tried the restrictive arts of government, and made law the protector, but not the tyrant of the people. We should then find that creatures, whose souls are held as dross, only wanted the hand of a refiner: we should then find that wretches, now stuck up for long tortures, lest luxury should feel a momentary pang, might, if properly treated, serve to sinew the state in times of danger; that as their faces are like ours, their hearts are so too; that few minds are so base as that perseverance cannot amend; that a man may see his last crime without dying for it; and that very little blood will serve to cement our security.

CHAPTER XXVIII

I HAD now been confined more than a fortnight, but had not since my arrival been visited by my dear Olivia, and I greatly longed to see her. Having communicated my wishes to my wife, the next morning the poor girl entered my apartment, leaning on her sister's arm. The change which I saw in her countenance struck me. The numberless graces that once resided there were now fled, and the hand of death seemed to have moulded every feature to alarm me. Her temples were sunk, her forehead was tense, and a fatal paleness sat upon her cheek.

"I am glad to see thee, my dear," cried I; "but why this dejection, Livy? I hope, my love, you have too great a regard for me to permit disappointment thus to undermine a life which I prize as my own. Be cheerful, child, and we may yet see happier days."

"You have ever, Sir," replied she, "been kind to me, and it adds to my pain that I shall never have an opportunity of sharing that happiness you promise. Happiness, I fear, is no longer reserved for me here; and I long to be rid of a place where

166

I have only found distress. Indeed, Sir, I wish you would make a proper submission to Mr Thornhill; it may in some measure induce him to pity you, and it will give me relief in dying."

"Never, child," replied I; "never will I be brought to acknowledge my daughter a prostitute; for though the world may look upon your offence with scorn, let it be mine to regard it as a mark of credulity, not of guilt. My dear, I am no way miserable in this place, however dismal it may seem; and be assured, that while you continue to bless me by living, he shall never have my consent to make you more wretched by marrying another."

After the departure of my daughter, my fellow-prisoner, who was by at this interview, sensibly enough expostulated on my obstinacy in refusing a submission which promised to give me freedom. He observed that the rest of my family was not to be sacrificed to the peace of one child alone, and she the only one who had offended me. "Besides," added he, "I don't know if it be just thus to obstruct the union of man and wife, which you do at present, by refusing to consent to a match you cannot hinder, but may render unhappy."

"Sir," replied I, "you are unacquainted with the man that oppresses us. I am very sensible that no submission I can make could procure me liberty even for an hour. I am told that even in this very room a debtor of his, no later than last year, died for want. But though my submission and approbation could transfer me from hence to the most beautiful apartment he is possessed of, yet I would grant neither, as something whispers me that it would be giving a sanction to adultery. While my daughter lives, no other marriage of his shall ever be legal in my eye. Were she removed, indeed, I should be the basest of men, from any resentment of my own, to attempt putting asunder those who wish for a union. No, villain as he is, I should then wish him married, to prevent the consequences of his future debaucheries. But now, should I not be the most cruel of all fathers, to sign an instrument which must send my child to the grave, merely to avoid a prison myself; and thus, to escape one pang, break my child's heart with a thousand?"

He acquiesced in the justice of this answer, but could not avoid observing, that he feared my daughter's life was already too much wasted to keep me long a prisoner. "However," continued he, "though you refuse to submit to the nephew, I hope you have no objections to laying your case before the uncle, who has the first character in the kingdom for everything that is just and good. I would advise you to send him a letter by the post, intimating all his nephew's ill-usage; and my life for it, that in three days you shall have an answer." I thanked him for the hint, and instantly set about complying; but I wanted paper, and unluckily all our money had been laid out that morning in provisions: however, he supplied me.

For the three ensuing days I was in a state of anxiety to know what reception my letter might meet with; but in the meantime was frequently solicited by my wife to submit to any conditions rather than remain here, and every hour received repeated accounts of the decline of my daughter's health. The third day and the fourth arrived, but I received no answer to my letter: the complaints of a stranger against a favourite nephew were no way likely to succeed; so that these hopes soon vanished like all my former. My mind, however, still supported itself, though confinement and bad air began to make a visible alteration in my health, and my arm that had suffered in the fire grew worse. My children, however, sat by me, and while I was stretched on my straw, read to me by turns, or listened and wept at my instructions. But my daughter's health declined faster than mine: every message from her contributed to increase my apprehensions and pain. The fifth morning after I had written the letter

168

which was sent to Sir William Thornhill, I was alarmed with an account that she was speechless. Now it was that confinement was truly painful to me; my soul was bursting from its prison to be near the pillow of my child, to comfort, to strengthen her, to receive her last wishes, and teach her soul the way to Heaven! Another account came: she was expiring, and I was debarred the small comfort of weeping by her. My fellow-prisoner, some time after, came with the last account. He bade me be patient: she was dead!——The next morning he returned, and found me with my two little ones, now my only companions, who were using all their innocent efforts to comfort me. They entreated to read to me, and bade me not to cry, for I was now too old to weep. "And is not my sister an angel now, papa?" cried the eldest; "and why, then, are you sorry for her? I wish I were an angel out of this frightful place, if my papa were with me."—"Yes," added my youngest darling, "Heaven, where my sister is, is a finer place than this, and there are none but good people there, and the people here are very bad."

Mr Jenkinson interrupted their harmless prattle by observing, that, now my daughter was no more, I should seriously think of the rest of my family, and attempt to save my own life, which was every day declining for want of necessaries and wholesome air. He added, that it was now incumbent on me to sacrifice any pride or resentment of my own to the welfare of those who depended on me for support; and that I was now, both by reason and justice, obliged to try to reconcile my landlord.

"Heaven be praised," replied I, "there is no pride left me now: I should detest my own heart if I saw either pride or resentment lurking there. On the contrary, as my oppressor has been once my parishioner, I hope one day to present him up an unpolluted soul at the eternal tribunal. No, Sir, I have no resentment now; and though he has taken from me what I held dearer than all his treasures, though he has wrung my heart,—for I am sick almost to fainting, very sick, my fellow-prisoner,—yet that shall never inspire me with vengeance. I am now willing to approve his marriage; and, if this submission can do him any pleasure, let him know that if I have done him any injury I am sorry for it."

Mr Jenkinson took pen and ink, and wrote down my submission nearly as I have expressed it, to which I signed my name. My son was employed to carry the letter to Mr Thornhill, who was then at his seat in the country. He went, and, in about six hours, returned with a verbal answer. He had some difficulty, he said, to get a sight of his landlord, as the servants were insolent and suspicious: but he accidentally saw him as he was going out upon business, preparing for his marriage, which was to be in three days. He continued to inform us, that he stept up in the humblest manner, and delivered the letter, which, when Mr Thornhill had read, he said that all submission was now too late and unnecessary; that he heard of our application to his uncle, which met with the contempt it deserved; and, as for the rest, that all future applications should be directed to his attorney, not to him. He observed, however, that as he had a very good opinion of the discretion of the two young ladies, they might have been the most agreeable intercessors.

"Well, Sir," said I to my fellow-prisoner, "you now discover the temper of the man that oppresses me. He can at once be facetious and cruel: but, let him use me as he will, I shall soon be free, in spite of all his bolts to restrain me. I am now drawing towards an abode that looks brighter as I approach it: this expectation cheers my afflictions, and though I leave an helpless family of orphans behind me, yet they will not be utterly forsaken: some friend, perhaps, will be found to assist them for the sake of their poor father, and some may charitably relieve them for the sake of their heavenly Father."

Just as I spoke, my wife, whom I had not seen that day before, appeared with looks of terror, and making efforts, but unable, to speak. "Why, my love," cried I, "why will you thus increase my afflictions by your own? What though no submissions can turn our severe master, though he has doomed me to die in this place of wretchedness, and though we have lost a darling child, yet still you will find comfort in your other children when I shall be no more."—"We have indeed lost," returned she, "a darling child. My Sophia, my dearest, is gone; snatched from us, carried off by ruffians!"—"How, madam," cried my fellow-prisoner, "Miss Sophia carried off by villains! sure it cannot be?"

She could only answer by a fixed look, and a flood of tears. But one of the prisoners' wives who was present, and came in with her, gave us a more distinct account: she informed us, that as my wife, my daughter, and herself were taking a walk together on the great road, a little way out of the village, a post-chaise and pair drove up to them, and instantly stopped; upon which a well-dressed man, but not Mr Thornhill, stepping out, clasped my daughter round the waist, and forcing her in, bade the postillion drive on, so that they were out of sight in a moment.

"Now," cried I, "the sum of my miseries is made up, nor is it in the power of anything on earth to give me another pang. What! not one left!—not to leave me one!—The monster!—The child that was next my heart!—she had the beauty of an angel, and almost the wisdom of an angel.—But support that woman, nor let her fall.—Not to leave me one!"

"Alas! my husband," said my wife, "you seem to want comfort even more than I. Our distresses are great, but I could bear this and more, if I saw you but easy. They may take away my children, and all the world, if they leave me but you."

My son, who was present, endeavoured to moderate our grief;

171

he bade us take comfort, for he hoped that we might still have reason to be thankful. "My child," cried I, "look round the world, and see if there be any happiness left me now. Is not every ray of comfort shut out, while all our bright prospects only lie beyond the grave?"—"My dear father," returned he, "I hope that there is still something that will give you an interval of satisfaction; for I have a letter from my brother George."— "What of him, child?" interrupted I; "does he know our misery? I hope my boy is exempt from any part of what his wretched family suffers?"—"Yes, Sir," returned he, "he is perfectly gay, cheerful, and happy. His letter brings nothing but good news; he is the favourite of his colonel, who promises to procure him the very next lieutenancy that becomes vacant."

"And are you sure of all this?" cried my wife: "are you sure that nothing ill has befallen my boy?"—"Nothing, indeed, madam," returned my son; "you shall see the letter, which will give you the highest pleasure; and if anything can procure you comfort, I am sure that will."—"But are you sure," still repeated she, "that the letter is from himself, and that he is really so happy?"—"Yes, madam," replied he, "it is certainly his, and he will one day be the credit and support of our family."—"Then, I thank Providence," cried she, "that my last letter to him has miscarried. Yes, my dear," continued she, turning to me, "I will now confess, that though the hand of Heaven is sore upon us in other instances, it has been favourable here. By the last letter I wrote my son, which was in the bitterness of anger, I desired him, upon his mother's blessing, and if he had the heart of a man, to see justice done his father and sister, and avenge our cause. But, thanks be to Him that directs all things, it has mis- carried, and I am at rest."—"Woman!" cried I, "thou hast done very ill, and at another time, my reproaches might have been more severe. Oh! what a tremendous gulf hast thou escaped,

172

that would have buried both thee and him in endless ruin; Providence, indeed, has here been kinder to us than we to ourselves. It has reserved that son to be the father and protector of my children when I shall be away. How unjustly did I complain of being stripped of every comfort, when still I hear that he is happy, and insensible of our afflictions; still kept in reserve to support his widowed mother, and to protect his brothers and sisters! But what sisters has he left? He has no sisters now: they are all gone, robbed from me, and I am undone."—"Father," interrupted my son, "I beg you will give me leave to read his letter —I know it will please you." Upon which, with my permission, he read as follows:

"HONOURED SIR,—I have called off my imagination a few moments from the pleasures that surround me, to fix it upon objects that are still more pleasing,—the dear little fireside at home. My fancy draws the harmless group, as listening to every line of this with great composure. I view those faces with delight, which never felt the deforming hand of ambition or distress! But, whatever your happiness may be at home, I am sure it will be some addition to it to hear that I am perfectly pleased with my situation, and every way happy here.

"Our regiment is countermanded, and is not to leave the kingdom. The colonel, who professes himself my friend, takes me with him to all companies where he is acquainted, and, after my first visit, I generally find myself received with increased respect upon repeating it. I danced last night with Lady G——, and could I forget you know whom, I might be perhaps successful. But it is my fate still to remember others, while I am myself forgotten by most of my absent friends; and in this number, I fear, Sir, that I must consider you; for I have long expected the pleasure of a letter from home, to no purpose. Olivia and Sophia too promised to write, but seem to have forgotten me. Tell them they are two arrant little baggages, and that I am at this moment in a most violent passion with them; yet still, I know not how, though I want to bluster a little, my heart is respondent only to softer emotions. Then tell them, Sir, that after all, I love them affectionately; and be assured of my ever remaining

Your dutiful Son."

"In all our miseries," cried I, "what thanks have we not to return, that one at least of our family is exempted from what we suffer! Heaven be his guard, and keep my boy thus happy, to be the support of his widowed mother, and the father of these two babes, which is all the patrimony I can now bequeath him! May he keep their innocence from the temptations of want, and be their conductor in the paths of honour!" I had scarce said these words, when a noise like that of a tumult seemed to proceed from the prison below: it died away soon after, and a clanking of fetters was heard along the passage that led to my apartment. The keeper of the prison entered, holding a man all bloody, wounded, and fettered with the heaviest irons. I looked with compassion on the wretch as he approached me, but with horror, when I found it was my own son. "My George! my George! and do I behold thee thus? Wounded—fettered? Is this thy happiness? is this the manner you return to me? Oh that this sight could break my heart at once, and let me die!"

"Where, Sir, is your fortitude?" returned my son, with an intrepid voice. "I must suffer; my life is forfeited, and let them take it."

I tried to restrain my passions for a few minutes in silence, but I thought I should have died with the effort. "Oh, my boy, my heart weeps to behold thee thus, and I cannot, cannot help it. In the moment that I thought thee blest, and prayed for thy safety, to behold thee thus again! Chained—wounded; and yet the death of the youthful is happy. But I am old, a very old man, and have lived to see this day! To see my children all untimely falling about me, while I continue a wretched survivor in the midst of ruin! May all the curses that ever sunk a soul fall heavy upon the murderer of my children! May he live, like me, to see——"

"Hold, Sir!" replied my son, "or I shall blush for thee. How, Sir! forgetful of your age, your holy calling, thus to arrogate the justice of Heaven, and fling those curses upward that must soon

174

descend to crush thy own grey head with destruction! No, Sir, let it be your care now to fit me for that vile death I must shortly suffer! to arm me with hope and resolution! to give me courage to drink of that bitterness which must shortly be my portion."

"My child, you must not die; I am sure no offence of thine can deserve so vile a punishment. My George could never be guilty of any crime to make his ancestors ashamed of him."

"Mine, Sir," returned my son, "is, I fear, an unpardonable one. When I received my mother's letter from home, I immediately came down, determined to punish the betrayer of our honour, and sent him an order to meet me, which he answered, not in person, but by despatching four of his domestics to seize me. I wounded one who first assaulted me, and I fear desperately; but the rest made me their prisoner. The coward is determined to put the law in execution against me; the proofs are undeniable; I have sent a challenge, and as I am the first transgressor upon the statute, I see no hope of pardon. But you have often charmed me with your lessons of fortitude; let me now, Sir, find them in your example."

"And, my son, you shall find them. I am now raised above this world, and all the pleasures it can produce. From this moment I break from my heart all the ties that held it down to earth, and will prepare to fit us both for eternity. Yes, my son, I will point out the way, and my soul shall guide yours in the ascent, for we will take our flight together. I now see, and am convinced, you can expect no pardon here; and I can only exhort you to seek it at that greatest tribunal where we both shall shortly answer. But let us not be niggardly in our exhortation, but let all our fellow-prisoners have a share. Good gaoler, let them be permitted to stand here while I attempt to improve them." Thus saying, I made an effort to rise from my straw, but wanted strength, and was able only to recline against the wall.

The prisoners assembled themselves according to my directions, for they loved to hear my counsel: my son and his mother supported me on either side; I looked and saw that none were wanting, and then addressed them with the following exhortation.

CHAPTER XXIX

"My friends, my children, and fellow-sufferers, when I reflect on the distribution of good and evil here below, I find that much has been given man to enjoy, yet still more to suffer. Though we should examine the whole world, we shall not find one man so happy as to have nothing left to wish for; but we daily see thousands who by suicide show us they have nothing left to hope. In this life, then, it appears that we cannot be entirely blest, but yet we may be completely miserable.

"Why man should thus feel pain; why our wretchedness should be requisite in the formation of universal felicity; why when all other systems are made perfect by the perfection of their subordinate parts, the great system should require for its perfection parts that are not only subordinate to others, but imperfect in themselves—these are questions that never can be explained, and might be useless if known. On this subject, Providence has thought fit to elude our curiosity, satisfied with granting us motives to consolation.

"In this situation man has called in the friendly assistance of

177

philosophy; and Heaven, seeing the incapacity of that to console him, has given him the aid of religion. The consolations of philosophy are very amusing, but often fallacious; it tells us that life is filled with comforts, if we will but enjoy them; and, on the other hand, that though we unavoidably have miseries here, life is short, and they will soon be over. Thus do these consolations destroy each other; for, if life is a place of comfort, its shortness must be misery, and if it be long, our griefs are protracted. Thus philosophy is weak: but religion comforts in a higher strain. Man is here, it tells us, fitting up his mind, and preparing it for another abode. When the good man leaves the body, and is all a glorious mind, he will find he has been making himself a heaven of happiness here; while the wretch that has been maimed and contaminated by his vices, shrinks from his body with terror, and finds that he has anticipated the vengeance of Heaven. To religion, then, we must hold, in every circumstance of life, for our truest comfort: for if already we are happy, it is a pleasure to think that we can make that happiness unending; and if we are miserable, it is very consoling to think that there is a place of rest. Thus, to the fortunate, religion holds out a continuance of bliss; to the wretched, a change from pain.

"But though religion is very kind to all men, it has promised peculiar rewards to the unhappy: the sick, the naked, the houseless, the heavy-laden, and the prisoner, have ever most frequent promises in our sacred law. The Author of our religion everywhere professes himself the wretch's friend, and, unlike the false ones of this world, bestows all his caresses upon the forlorn. The unthinking have censured this as partiality, as a preference without merit to deserve it. But they never reflect, that it is not in the power even of Heaven itself to make the offer of unceasing felicity as great a gift to the happy as to the miserable. To the first, eternity is but a single blessing, since at most

178

it but increases what they already possess. To the latter, it is a double advantage; for it diminishes their pain here, and rewards them with heavenly bliss hereafter.

"But Providence is in another respect kinder to the poor than to the rich, for as it thus makes the life after death more desirable, so it smoothes the passage there. The wretched have had a long familiarity with every face of terror. The man of sorrows lays himself quietly down, without possessions to regret, and but few ties to stop his departure: he feels only nature's pang in the final separation, and this is no way greater than he has often fainted under before; for, after a certain degree of pain, every new breach that death opens in the constitution nature kindly covers with insensibility.

"Thus Providence has given the wretched two advantages over the happy in this life,—greater felicity in dying, and in heaven all that superiority of pleasure which arises from contrasted enjoyment. And this superiority, my friends, is no small advantage, and seems to be one of the pleasures of the poor man in the parable; for though he was already in heaven, and felt all the raptures it could give, yet it was mentioned as an addition to his happiness, that he had once been wretched, and now was comforted; that he had known what it was to be miserable, and now felt what it was to be happy.

"Thus, my friends, you see religion does what philosophy could never do: it shows the equal dealings of Heaven to the happy and the unhappy, and levels all human enjoyments to nearly the same standard. It gives to both rich and poor the same happiness hereafter, and equal hopes to aspire after it; but if the rich have the advantage of enjoying pleasure here, the poor have the endless satisfaction of knowing what it was once to be miserable, when crowned with endless felicity hereafter; and even though this should be called a small advantage, yet, being an eternal one, it must make up by duration what the temporal happiness of the great may have exceeded by intenseness.

"These are, therefore, the consolations which the wretched have peculiar to themselves, and in which they are above the rest of mankind: in other respects, they are below them. They who would know the miseries of the poor, must see life and endure it. To declaim on the temporal advantages they enjoy, is only repeating what none either believe or practice. The men who have the necessaries of living are not poor; and they who want them must be miserable. Yes, my friends, we must be miserable. No vain efforts of a refined imagination can soothe the wants of nature, can give elastic sweetness to the dank vapour of a dungeon, or ease to the throbbings of a broken heart. Let the philosopher from his couch of softness tell us that we can resist all these: alas! the effort by which we resist them is still the greatest pain. Death is slight, and any man may sustain it; but torments are dreadful, and these no man can endure.

"To us then, my friends, the promises of happiness in heaven should be peculiarly dear; for if our reward be in this life alone, we are then, indeed, of all men the most miserable. When I look round these gloomy walls, made to terrify as well as to confine us; this light, that only serves to show the horrors of the place; those shackles, that tyranny has imposed, or crime made necessary; when I survey these emaciated looks, and hear those groans—oh, my friends, what a glorious exchange would heaven be for these! To fly through regions unconfined as air—to bask in the sunshine of eternal bliss—to carol over endless hymns of praise—to have no master to threaten or insult us, but the form of Goodness himself for ever in our eyes!—when I think of these things, death becomes the messenger of very glad tidings; when I think of these things, his sharpest arrow becomes the staff of

180

my support; when I think of these things, what is there in life worth having? when I think of these things, what is there that should not be spurned away? Kings in their palaces should groan for such advantages; but we, humbled as we are, should yearn for them.

"And shall these things be ours? Ours they will certainly be, if we but try for them; and, what is a comfort, we are shut out from many temptations that would retard our pursuit. Only let us try for them, and they will certainly be ours; and, what is still a comfort, shortly too: for if we look back on past life, it appears but a very short span, and whatever we may think of the rest of life, it will yet be found of less duration; as we grow older, the days seem to grow shorter, and our intimacy with Time ever lessens the perception of his stay. Then let us take comfort now, for we shall soon be at our journey's end; we shall soon lay down the heavy burden laid by Heaven upon us; and though death, the only friend of the wretched, for a little while mocks the weary traveller with the view, and like his horizon still flies before him; yet the time will certainly and shortly come, when we shall cease from our toil; when the luxurious great ones of the world shall no more tread us to the earth; when we shall think with pleasure of our sufferings below; when we shall be surrounded with all our friends, or such as deserved our friendship; when our bliss shall be unutterable, and still, to crown all, unending."

CHAPTER XXX

WHEN I had thus finished, and my audience was retired, the gaoler, who was one of the most humane of his profession, hoped I would not be displeased, as what he did was but his duty, observing that he must be obliged to remove my son into a stronger cell, but that he should be permitted to revisit me every morning. I thanked him for his clemency, and grasping my boy's hand, bade him farewell, and be mindful of the great duty that was before him.

I again therefore laid me down, and one of my little ones sat by my bedside reading, when Mr Jenkinson entering, informed me that there was news of my daughter; for that she was seen by a person about two hours before in a strange gentleman's company, and that they had stopped at a neighbouring village for refreshment, and seemed as if returning to town. He had scarcely delivered this news when the gaoler came, with looks of haste and pleasure, to inform me that my daughter was found. Moses came running in a moment after, crying out that his sister Sophy was below, and coming up with our old friend Mr Burchell.

Just as he delivered this news, my dearest girl entered, and, with looks almost wild with pleasure, ran to kiss me, in a transport of affection. Her mother's tears and silence also showed her pleasure. "Here, papa," cried the charming girl, "here is the brave man to whom I owe my delivery; to this gentleman's intrepidity I am indebted for my happiness and safety——" A kiss from Mr Burchell, whose pleasure seemed even greater than hers, interrupted what she was going to add.

"Ah! Mr Burchell," cried I, "this is but a wretched habitation you now find us in; and we are now very different from what you last saw us. You were ever our friend: we have long discovered our errors with regard to you, and repented of our ingratitude. After the vile usage you then received at my hands, I am almost ashamed to behold your face; yet I hope you'll forgive me, as I was deceived by a base ungenerous wretch, who, under the mask of friendship, has undone me."

"It is impossible," cried Mr Burchell, "that I should forgive you, as you never deserved my resentment. I partly saw your delusion then, and as it was out of my power to restrain, I could only pity it."

"It was ever my conjecture," cried I, "that your mind was noble; but now I find it so. But tell me, my dear child, how thou hast been relieved, or who the ruffians were who carried thee away?"

"Indeed, Sir," replied she, "as to the villain who carried me off, I am yet ignorant. For, as my mamma and I were walking out, he came behind us, and almost before I could call for help, forced me into the post-chaise, and in an instant the horses drove away. I met several on the road, to whom I cried out for assistance, but they disregarded my entreaties. In the meantime, the ruffian himself used every art to hinder me from crying out: he flattered and threatened by turns, and swore that, if I continued but silent, he intended no harm. In the meantime, I had broken the canvas that he had drawn up, and whom should I perceive at some distance but your old friend Mr Burchell, walking along with his usual swiftness, with the great stick for which we used so much to ridicule him. As soon as we came within hearing, I called out to him by name, and entreated his help. I repeated my exclamations several times, upon which, with a very loud voice, he bid the postillion stop; but the boy took no notice, but drove on with still greater speed. I now thought he could never overtake us, when, in less than a minute, I saw Mr Burchell come running up by the side of the horses, and, with one blow, knock the postillion to the ground. The horses, when he was fallen, soon stopped of themselves, and the ruffian, stepping out, with oaths and menaces, drew his sword, and ordered him, at his peril, to retire; but Mr Burchell, running up, shivered his sword to pieces, and then pursued him for nearly a quarter of a mile; but he made his escape. I was at this time come out myself, willing to assist my deliverer; but he soon returned to me in triumph. The postillion, who was recovered, was going to make his escape too; but Mr Burchell ordered him at his peril to mount again and drive back to town. Finding it impossible to resist, he reluctantly complied, though the wound he had received seemed, to me at least, to be dangerous. He continued to complain of the pain as we drove along, so that he at last excited Mr Burchell's compassion, who, at my request, exchanged him for another, at an inn where we called on our return."

"Welcome, then," cried I, "my child! and thou, her gallant deliverer, a thousand welcomes! Though our cheer is but wretched, yet our hearts are ready to receive you. And now, Mr Burchell, as you have delivered my girl, if you think her a recompense, she is yours: if you can stoop to an alliance with a family so poor as mine, take her; obtain her consent,—as I know you have her heart,—and you have mine. And let me tell you, Sir, that I give you no small treasure: she has been celebrated for beauty, it is true, but that is not my meaning,—I give you up a treasure in her mind."

"But I suppose, Sir," cried Mr Burchell, "that you are apprised of my circumstances, and of my incapacity to support her as she deserves?"

"If your present objection," replied I, "be meant as an evasion of my offer, I desist; but I know no man so worthy to deserve her as you; and if I could give her thousands, and thousands sought her from me, yet my honest brave Burchell should be my dearest choice."

To all this his silence alone seemed to give a mortifying refusal: and, without the least reply to my offer, he demanded if he could not be furnished with refreshments from the next inn; to which being answered in the affirmative, he ordered them to send in the best dinner that could be provided upon such short notice. He bespoke also a dozen of their best wine, and some cordials for me; adding, with a smile, that he would stretch a little for once, and, though in a prison, asserted he was never better disposed to be merry. The waiter soon made his appearance with preparations for dinner; a table was lent us by the gaoler, who seemed remarkably assiduous; the wine was disposed in order, and two very well dressed dishes were brought in.

My daughter had not yet heard of her poor brother's melancholy situation, and we all seemed unwilling to damp her cheerfulness by the relation. But it was in vain that I attempted to appear cheerful: the circumstances of my unfortunate son broke through all efforts to dissemble; so that I was at last obliged to damp our mirth by relating his misfortunes, and wishing that he might be permitted to share with us in this little interval of satisfaction. After my guests were recovered from the consternation my account had produced, I requested also that Mr Jenkinson, a fellow-prisoner, might be admitted, and the gaoler granted my request with an air of unusual submission. The clanking of my son's irons was no sooner heard along the passage, than his sister ran impatiently to meet him, while Mr Burchell, in the meantime, asked me if my son's name was George; to which replying in the affirmative, he still continued silent. As soon as my boy entered the room, I could perceive he regarded Mr Burchell with a look of astonishment and reverence. "Come on," cried I, "my son; though we are fallen very low, yet Providence has been pleased to grant us some small relaxation from pain. Thy sister is restored to us, and there is her deliverer: to that brave man it is that I am indebted for yet having a daughter: give him, my boy, the hand of friendship; he deserves our warmest gratitude."

My son seemed all this while regardless of what I said, and still continued fixed at respectful distance. "My dear brother," cried his sister, "why don't you thank my good deliverer? the brave should ever love each other."

He still continued his silence and astonishment, till our guest at last perceived himself to be known, and, assuming all his native dignity, desired my son to come forward. Never before had I seen anything so truly majestic as the air he assumed on this occasion. The greatest object in the universe, says a certain philosopher, is a good man struggling with adversity; yet there is still a greater, which is the good man that comes to relieve it. After he had regarded my son for some time with a superior air—"I again find," said he, "unthinking boy, that the same crime——" But here he was interrupted by one of the gaoler's servants, who came to inform us that a person of distinction, who had driven into town with a chariot and several attendants, sent his respects to the gentleman that was with us, and begged to know when he should think proper to be waited upon. "Bid the fellow wait," cried our guest, "till I shall have leisure to receive him;" and then turning to my son, "I again find, Sir," proceeded he, "that you are guilty of the same offence for which you once had my reproof, and for which the law is now preparing its justest punishments. You imagine, perhaps, that a contempt for your own life gives you a right to take that of another: but where, Sir, is the difference between a duellist, who hazards a life of no value, and the murderer who acts with greater security? Is it any diminution of the gamester's fraud, when he alleges that he has staked a counter?"

"Alas, Sir," cried I, "whoever you are, pity the poor misguided creature; for what he has done was in obedience to a deluded mother, who, in the bitterness of her resentment, required him, upon her blessing, to avenge her quarrel. Here, Sir, is the letter, which will serve to convince you of her imprudence, and diminish his guilt."

He took the letter, and hastily read it over. "This," says he, "though not a perfect excuse, is such a palliation of his fault as induces me to forgive him. And now, Sir," continued he, kindly taking my son by the hand, "I see you are surprised at finding me here; but I have often visited prisons upon occasions less interesting. I am now come to see justice done a worthy man, for whom I have the most sincere esteem. I have long been a disguised spectator of thy father's benevolence. I have, at his little dwelling, enjoyed respect uncontaminated by flattery; and have received that happiness that courts could not give, from the amusing simplicity around his fireside. My nephew has been apprised of my intentions of coming here, and, I find, is arrived. It would be wronging him and you to condemn him without examination: if there be injury, there shall be redress; and this I may say, without boasting, that none have ever taxed the injustice of Sir William Thornhill."

We now found the personage whom we had so long entertained as an harmless amusing companion was no other than the celebrated Sir William Thornhill, to whose virtues and singularities scarce any were strangers. The poor Mr Burchell was in reality a man of large fortune and great interest, to whom senates listened with applause, and whom party heard with conviction: who was the friend of his country, but loyal to his king. My poor wife, recollecting her former familiarity, seemed to shrink with apprehension; but Sophia, who a few moments before thought him her own, now perceiving the immense distance to which he was removed by fortune, was unable to conceal her tears.

"Ah! Sir," cried my wife, with a piteous aspect, "how is it possible that I can ever have your forgiveness? The slights you received from me the last time I had the honour of seeing you at our house, and the jokes which I audaciously threw out—these jokes, sir, I fear, can never be forgiven."

"My dear good lady," returned he with a smile, "if you had your joke, I had my answer: I'll leave it to all the company if mine were not as good as yours. To say the truth, I know nobody whom I am disposed to be angry with at present, but the fellow who so frighted my little girl here. I had not even time to examine the rascal's person so as to describe him in an advertisement. Can you tell me, Sophia, my dear, whether you should know him again?"

"Indeed, sir," replied she, "I can't be positive; yet now I recollect, he had a large mark over one of his eyebrows."—"I ask pardon, madam," interrupted Jenkinson, who was by, "but be so good as to inform me if the fellow wore his own red hair?"—"Yes, I think so," cried Sophia. "And did your honour," continued he, turning to Sir William, "observe the length of his legs?"—"I can't be sure of their length," cried the Baronet, "but I am convinced of their swiftness; for he outran me, which is what I thought few men in the kingdom could have done."—"Please your honour," cried Jenkinson, "I know the man: it is certainly the same: the best runner in England; he has beaten Pinwire of Newcastle: Timothy Baxter is his name; I know him perfectly, and the very place of his retreat this moment. If your honour will bid Mr Gaoler let two of his men go with me, I'll engage to produce him to you in an hour at farthest." Upon this the gaoler was called, who instantly appearing, Sir William demanded if he knew him. "Yes, please your honour," replied the gaoler, "I know Sir William Thornhill well, and everybody that knows anything of him will desire to know more of him." "Well, then," said the Baronet, "my request is, that you will permit this man and two of your servants to go upon a message by my authority; and as I am in the commission of the peace, I undertake to secure you."—"Your promise is sufficient," replied the other, "and you may, at a minute's warning, send them over England whenever your honour thinks fit."

In pursuance of the gaoler's compliance, Jenkinson was despatched in search of Timothy Baxter, while we were amused with the assiduity of our youngest boy Bill, who had just come in and climbed up Sir William's neck, in order to kiss him. His mother was immediately going to chastise his familiarity, but the worthy man prevented her; and taking the child, all ragged as he was, upon his knee, "What, Bill, you chubby rogue," cried he, "do you remember your old friend Burchell? and Dick, too, my honest veteran, are you here? you shall find I have not forgot you." So saying, he gave each a large piece of ginger-bread, which the poor fellows ate very heartily, as they had got that morning but a very scanty breakfast.

We now sat down to dinner, which was almost cold; but previously, my arm still continuing painful, Sir William wrote a prescription, for he had made the study of physic his amusement, and was more than moderately skilled in the profession: this being sent to an apothecary who lived in the place, my arm was dressed, and I found almost instantaneous relief. We were waited upon at dinner by the gaoler himself, who was willing to do our guest all the honour in his power. But before we had well dined, another message was brought from his nephew, desiring permission to appear in order to vindicate his innocence and honour; with which request the Baronet complied, and desired Mr Thornhill to be introduced.

CHAPTER XXXI

Mr Thornhill made his appearance with a smile, which he seldom wanted, and was going to embrace his uncle, which the other repulsed with an air of disdain. "No fawning, Sir, at present," cried the Baronet, with a look of severity; "the only way to my heart is by the road of honour; but here I only see complicated instances of falsehood, cowardice, and oppression. How is it, Sir, that this poor man, for whom I know you professed a friendship, is used thus hardly? His daughter vilely seduced as a recompense for his hospitality, and he himself thrown into prison, perhaps but for resenting the insult? His son, too, whom you feared to face as a man——"

"Is it possible, Sir," interrupted his nephew, "that my uncle should object that as a crime, which his repeated instructions alone have persuaded me to avoid?"

"Your rebuke," cried Sir William, "is just; you have acted, in this instance, prudently and well, though not quite as your father would have done: my brother, indeed was the soul of hon-

191

our; but thou——Yes, you have acted, in this instance, perfectly right, and it has my warmest approbation."

"And I hope," said his nephew, "that the rest of my conduct will not be found to deserve censure. I appeared, Sir, with this gentleman's daughter at some places of public amusement: thus, what was levity, scandal called by a harsher name, and it was reported I had debauched her. I waited on her father in person, willing to clear the thing to his satisfaction, and he received me only with insult and abuse. As for the rest, with regard to his being here, my attorney and steward can best inform you, as I commit the management of business entirely to them. If he has contracted debts, and is unwilling, or even unable to pay them, it is their business to proceed in this manner: and I see no hardship or injustice in pursuing the most legal means of redress."

"If this," cried Sir William, "be as you have stated it, there is nothing unpardonable in your offence; and though your conduct might have been more generous in not suffering this gentleman to be oppressed by subordinate tyranny, yet it has been at least equitable."

"He cannot contradict a single particular," replied the 'Squire; "I defy him to do so; and several of my servants are ready to attest what I say. Thus, Sir," continued he, finding that I was silent, for in fact I could not contradict him—"thus, Sir, my own innocence is vindicated: but though, at your entreaty, I am ready to forgive this gentleman every other offence, yet his attempts to lessen me in your esteem excite a resentment that I cannot govern. And this, too, at a time when his son was actually preparing to take away my life,—this, I say, was such guilt, that I am determined to let the law take its course. I have here the challenge that was sent me, and two witnesses to prove it: one of my servants has been wounded dangerously; and even though my uncle himself should dissuade me, which I know he

192

will not, yet I will see public justice done, and he shall suffer for it."

"Thou monster!" cried my wife, "hast thou not had vengeance enough already, but must my poor boy feel thy cruelty? I hope that good Sir William will protect us; for my son is as innocent as a child: I am sure he is, and never did harm to man."

"Madam," replied the good man, "your wishes for his safety are not greater than mine; but I am sorry to find his guilt too plain; and if my nephew persists——" But the appearance of Jenkinson and the gaoler's two servants now called off our attention, who entered, hauling in a tall man, very genteelly dressed, and answering the description already given of the ruffian who had carried off my daughter. "Here," cried Jenkinson, pulling him in, "here we have him; and if ever there was a candidate for Tyburn, this is one."

The moment Mr Thornhill perceived the prisoner, and Jenkinson who had him in custody, he seemed to shrink back with terror. His face became pale with conscious guilt, and he would have withdrawn, but Jenkinson, who perceived his design, stopped him. "What, 'Squire," cried he, "are you ashamed of your two old acquaintances, Jenkinson and Baxter? But this is the way that all great men forget their friends, though I am resolved we will not forget you. Our prisoner, please your honour," continued he, turning to Sir William, "has already confessed all. This is the gentleman reported to be so dangerously wounded. He declares that it was Mr Thornhill who first put him upon this affair; that he gave him the clothes he now wears, to appear like a gentleman, and furnished him with the post-chaise. The plan was laid between them, that he should carry off the young lady to a place of safety, and that there he should threaten and terrify her; but Mr Thornhill was to come in, in the meantime, as if by accident, to her rescue; and that they should fight awhile, and then he was to run off,—by which Mr Thornhill would have the better opportunity of gaining her affections himself, under the character of her defender."

Sir William remembered the coat to have been worn by his nephew, and all the rest the prisoner himself confirmed by a more circumstantial account: concluding, that Mr Thornhill had often declared to him that he was in love with both sisters at the same time.

"Heavens!" cried Sir William, "what a viper have I been fostering in my bosom! And so fond of public justice, too, as he seemed to be! But he shall have it; secure him, Mr Gaoler—Yet, hold! I fear there is not legal evidence to detain him."

Upon this, Mr Thornhill, with the utmost humility, entreated that two such abandoned wretches might not be admitted as evidences against him, but that his servants should be examined. "Your servants!" replied Sir William. "Wretch! call them yours no longer: but come, let us hear what those fellows have to say; let his butler be called."

When the butler was introduced, he soon perceived by his former master's looks that all his power was now over. "Tell me," cried Sir William, sternly, "have you ever seen your master and that fellow dressed up in his clothes, in company together?" —"Yes, please your honour," cried the butler, "a thousand times: he was the man that always brought him his ladies."—"How!" interrupted young Mr Thornhill, "this to my face?" "Yes," replied the butler, "or to any man's face. To tell you a truth, Master Thornhill, I never either loved or liked you, and I don't care if I tell you now a piece of my mind."—"Now, then," cried Jenkinson, "tell his honour whether you know anything of me."— "I can't say," replied the butler, "that I know much good of you. The night that gentleman's daughter was deluded to our house,

194

you were one of them."—"So then," cried Sir William, "I find you have brought a very fine witness to prove your innocence: thou stain to humanity! to associate with such wretches! But," continuing his examination, "you tell me, Mr Butler, that this was the person who brought him this old gentleman's daughter."—"No, please your honour," replied the butler, "he did not bring her, for the 'Squire himself undertook that business; but he brought the priest that pretended to marry them."—"It is but too true," cried Jenkinson; "I cannot deny it; that was the employment assigned me, and I confess it to my confusion."

"Good heavens," exclaimed the Baronet, "how every new discovery of his villainy alarms me! All his guilt is now too plain, and I find his present prosecution was dictated by tyranny, cowardice, and revenge. At my request, Mr Gaoler, set this young officer, now your prisoner, free, and trust to me for the consequences. I'll make it my business to set the affair in a proper light to my friend the magistrate, who has committed him. But where is the unfortunate young lady herself? Let her appear to confront this wretch: I long to know by what arts he has seduced her. Entreat her to come in. Where is she?"

"Ah! Sir," said I, "that question stings me to the heart: I was once indeed happy in a daughter, but her miseries——" Another interruption here prevented me; for who should make her appearance but Miss Arabella Wilmot, who was next day to have been married to Mr Thornhill. Nothing could equal her surprise at seeing Sir William and his nephew here before her; for her arrival was quite accidental. It happened that she and the old gentleman, her father, were passing through the town, on the way to her aunt's, who had insisted that her nuptials with Mr Thornhill should be consummated at her house; but stopping for refreshment, they put up at an inn at the other end of the town. It was there, from the window, that the young lady happened to observe one of my little boys playing in the street, and instantly sending a footman to bring the child to her, she learned from him some account of our misfortunes; but was still kept ignorant of young Mr Thornhill's being the cause. Though her father made several remonstrances on the impropriety of going to a prison to visit us, yet they were ineffectual; she desired the child to conduct her, which he did, and it was thus she surprised us at a juncture so unexpected.

Nor can I go on without a reflection on those accidental meetings, which though they happen every day, seldom excite our surprise but upon some extraordinary occasion. To what a fortuitous concurrence do we not owe every pleasure and convenience of our lives! How many seeming accidents must unite before we can be clothed or fed! The peasant must be disposed to labour, the shower must fall, the wind fill the merchant's sail, or numbers must want the usual supply.

We all continued silent for some moments, while my charming pupil, which was the name I generally gave this young lady, united in her looks compassion and astonishment, which gave new finishings to her beauty.—"Indeed, my dear Mr Thornhill," cried she to the 'Squire, who she supposed was come here to succour, and not to oppress us, "I take it a little unkindly that you should come here without me, or never inform me of the situation of a family so dear to us both: you know I should take as much pleasure in contributing to the relief of my reverend old master here, whom I shall ever esteem, as you can. But I find that, like your uncle, you take a pleasure in doing good in secret."

"He find pleasure in doing good!" cried Sir William, interrupting her. "No, my dear, his pleasures are as base as he is. You see in him, madam, as complete a villain as ever disgraced humanity. A wretch, who, after having deluded this poor man's

196

daughter, after plotting against the innocence of her sister, has thrown the father into prison, and the eldest son into fetters because he had the courage to face her betrayer. And give me leave, madam, now to congratulate you upon an escape from the embraces of such a monster."

"O goodness!" cried the lovely girl, "how have I been deceived! Mr Thornhill informed me for certain that this gentleman's eldest son, Captain Primrose, was gone off to America with his new-married lady."

"My sweetest miss," cried my wife, "he has told you nothing but falsehood. My son George never left the kingdom, nor ever was married. Though you have forsaken him, he has always loved you too well to think of anybody else; and I have heard him say he would die a bachelor for your sake." She then proceeded to expatiate upon the sincerity of her son's passion: she set his duel with Mr Thornhill in a proper light; from thence she made a rapid digression to the 'Squire's debaucheries, his pretended marriages, and ended with a most insulting picture of his cowardice.

"Good heavens!" cried Miss Wilmot, "how very near have I been to the brink of ruin! But how great is my pleasure to have escaped it! Ten thousand falsehoods has this gentleman told me! He had at last art enough to persuade me, that my promise to the only man I esteemed was no longer binding, since he had been unfaithful. By his falsehoods I was taught to detest one equally brave and generous!"

But by this time my son was freed from the encumbrances of justice, as the person supposed to be wounded was detected to be an impostor. Mr Jenkinson, also, who had acted as his valet-de-chambre, had dressed up his hair, and furnished him with whatever was necessary to make a genteel appearance. He now therefore entered, handsomely dressed in his regimentals; and, without vanity (for I am above it), he appeared as handsome a fellow as ever wore a military dress. As he entered, he made Miss Wilmot a modest and distant bow, for he was not as yet acquainted with the change which the eloquence of his mother had wrought in his favour. But no decorums could restrain the impatience of his blushing mistress to be forgiven. Her tears, her looks, all contributed to discover the real sensations of her heart, for having forgotten her former promise, and having suffered herself to be deluded by an impostor. My son appeared amazed at her condescension, and could scarce believe it real. —"Sure, madam," cried he, "this is but delusion! I can never have merited this! To be blessed thus is to be too happy."—"No, sir," replied she; "I have been deceived, basely deceived, else nothing could have ever made me unjust to my promise. You know my friendship—you have long known it—but forget what I have done, and as you once had my warmest vows of constancy, you shall now have them repeated; and be assured, that, if your Arabella cannot be yours, she shall never be another's." —"And no other's you shall be," cried Sir William, "if I have any influence with your father."

This hint was sufficient for my son Moses, who immediately flew to the inn where the old gentleman was, to inform him of every circumstance that had happened. But in the meantime, the 'Squire, perceiving that he was on every side undone, now finding that no hopes were left from flattery or dissimulation, concluded that his wisest way would be to turn and face his pursuers. Thus, laying aside all shame, he appeared the open, hardy villain. "I find, then," cried he, "that I am to expect no justice here; but I am resolved it shall be done me. You shall know, Sir," turning to Sir William, "I am no longer a poor dependant upon your favours. I scorn them. Nothing can keep Miss Wilmot's fortune from me, which, I thank her father's assiduity, is pretty large. The articles, and a bond for her fortune, are signed, and safe in my possession. It was her fortune, not her person, that induced me to wish for this match; and, possessed of the one, let who will take the other."

This was an alarming blow. Sir William was sensible of the justice of his claims, for he had been instrumental in drawing up the marriage articles himself. Miss Wilmot, therefore, perceiving that her fortune was irretrievably lost, turning to my son, she asked if the loss of fortune could lessen her value to him? "Though fortune," said she, "is out of my power, at least I have my hand to give."

"And that, madam," cried her real lover, "was indeed all that you ever had to give; at least all that I ever thought worth the acceptance. And now I protest, my Arabella, by all that's happy, your want of fortune this moment increases my pleasure, as it serves to convince my sweet girl of my sincerity."

Mr Wilmot now entering, he seemed not a little pleased at the danger his daughter had just escaped, and readily consented to a dissolution of the match. But finding that her fortune, which was secured to Mr Thornhill by bond, would not be given up, nothing could exceed his disappointment. He now saw that his money must all go to enrich one who had no fortune of his own. He could bear his being a rascal, but to want an equivalent to his daughter's fortune was wormwood. He sat, therefore, for some minutes employed in the most mortifying speculations, till Sir William attempted to lessen his anxiety. "I must confess, Sir," cried he, "that your present disappointment does not entirely displease me. Your immoderate passion for wealth is now justly punished. But though the young lady cannot be rich, she has still a competence sufficient to give content. Here you see an honest young soldier, who is willing to take her without fortune: they have long loved each other; and for the friendship I

199

bear his father, my interest shall not be wanting in his promotion. Leave, then, that ambition which disappoints you, and for once admit that happiness which courts your acceptance."

"Sir William," replied the old gentleman, "be assured I never yet forced her inclinations, nor will I now. If she still continues to love this young gentleman, let her have him, with all my heart. There is still, thank Heaven, some fortune left, and your promise will make it something more. Only let my old friend here" (meaning me) "give me a promise of settling six thousand pounds upon my girl if ever he should come to his fortune, and I am ready, this night, to be the first to join them together."

As it now remained with me to make the young couple happy, I readily made a promise of making the settlement he required; which, to one who had such little expectations as I, was no great favour. We had now, therefore, the satisfaction of seeing them fly into each other's arms in a transport. "After all my misfortunes," cried my son George, "to be thus rewarded! Sure this is more than I could ever have presumed to hope for. To be possessed of all that's good, and after such an interval of pain! My warmest wishes could never rise so high!"

"Yes, my George," returned his lovely bride, "now let the wretch take my fortune; since you are happy without it, so am I. Oh, what an exchange have I made,—from the basest of men, to the dearest, best! Let him enjoy our fortune, I can now be happy even in indigence."—"And I promise you," cried the 'Squire, with a malicious grin, "that I shall be very happy with what you despise."—"Hold, hold, sir," cried Jenkinson, "there are two words to that bargain. As for the lady's fortune, Sir, you shall never touch a single stiver of it. Pray, your honour," continued he to Sir William, "can the 'Squire have this lady's fortune if he be married to another?"—"How can you make such a simple demand?" replied the Baronet: "undoubtedly he cannot."—"I am sorry for that," cried Jenkinson; "for as this gentleman and I have been old fellow-sporters, I have a friendship for him. But I must declare, well as I love him, that this contract is not worth a tobacco-stopper, for he is married already."—"You lie, like a rascal!" returned the 'Squire, who seemed roused by this insult; "I never was legally married to any woman."

"Indeed, begging your honour's pardon," replied the other, "you were: and I hope you will show a proper return of friendship to your own honest Jenkinson, who brings you a wife; and if the company restrain their curiosity a few minutes, they shall see her." So saying, he went off, with his usual celerity, and left us all unable to form any probable conjecture as to his design. "Ay, let him go," cried the 'Squire; "whatever else I may have done, I defy him there. I am too old now to be frightened with squibs."

"I am surprised," said the Baronet, "what the fellow can intend by this. Some low piece of humour, I suppose!"—"Perhaps, Sir," replied I, "he may have a more serious meaning. For when we reflect on the various schemes this gentleman has laid to seduce innocence, perhaps some one more artful than the rest has been found able to deceive him. When we consider what numbers he has ruined, how many parents now feel, with anguish, the infamy and the contamination which he has brought into their families, it would not surprise me if some one of them—— Amazement! Do I see my lost daughter? Do I hold her? It is, it is my life, my happiness! I thought thee lost, my Olivia, yet still I hold thee—and still thou shalt live to bless me." The warmest transports of the fondest lover were not greater than mine, when I saw him introduce my child, and held my daughter in my arms, whose silence only spoke her raptures.

"And art thou returned to me, my darling," cried I, "to be my comfort in age?"—"That she is," cried Jenkinson; "and make much of her, for she is your own honourable child, and as honest a woman as any in the whole room, let the other be who she will. And as for you, 'Squire, as sure as you stand there, this young lady is your lawful wedded wife: and to convince you that I speak nothing but the truth, here is the license by which you were married together." So saying, he put the license into the Baronet's hands, who read it, and found it perfect in every respect. "And now, gentlemen," continued he, "I find you are surprised at all this; but a few words will explain the difficulty. That there 'Squire of renown, for whom I have a great friendship (but that's between ourselves), has often employed me in doing odd little things for him. Among the rest, he commissioned me to procure him a false license and a false priest, in order to deceive this young lady. But as I was very much his friend, what did I do, but went and got a true license and a true priest, and married them both as fast as the cloth could make them. Perhaps you'll think it was generosity that made me do all this; but no; to my shame I confess it, my only design was to keep the license, and let the 'Squire know that I could prove it upon him whenever I thought proper, and so make him come down whenever I wanted money." A burst of pleasure now seemed to fill the whole apartment; our joy reached even to the common room, where the prisoners themselves sympathised,

> . . . And shook their chains
> In transport and rude harmony.

Happiness was expanded upon every face, and even Olivia's cheek seemed flushed with pleasure. To be thus restored to reputation, to friends, and fortune at once, was a rapture sufficient to stop the progress of decay, and restore former health and vivacity. But, perhaps, among all, there was not one who felt sincerer pleasure than I. Still holding the dear loved child in my arms, I asked my heart if these transports were not delusions. "How could you," cried I, turning to Mr Jenkinson, "how could you add to my miseries by the story of her death? But it matters not; my pleasure at finding her again is more than a recompense for the pain."

"As to your question," replied Jenkinson, "that is easily answered. I thought the only probable means of freeing you from prison was by submitting to the 'Squire, and consenting to his marriage with the other young lady. But these you had vowed never to grant while your daughter was living: there was therefore no other method to bring things to bear, but by persuading you that she was dead. I prevailed on your wife to join in the deceit, and we have not had a fit opportunity of undeceiving you till now."

In the whole assembly now there appeared only two faces that did not glow with transport. Mr Thornhill's assurance had entirely forsaken him; he now saw the gulf of infamy and want before him, and trembled to take the plunge. He therefore fell on his knees before his uncle, and in a voice of piercing misery implored compassion. Sir William was going to spurn him away, but at my request he raised him, and, after pausing a few moments, "Thy vices, crimes, and ingratitude," cried he, "deserve no tenderness; yet thou shalt not be entirely forsaken,—a bare competence shall be supplied to support the wants of life, but not its follies. This young lady, thy wife, shall be put in possession of a third part of that fortune which once was thine, and from her tenderness alone thou art to expect any extraordinary supplies for the future." He was going to express his gratitude for such kindness in a set speech; but the Baronet prevented him, by bidding him not aggravate his meanness, which was already but too apparent. He ordered him at the same time to be gone, and from all his former domestics to choose one, such as he should think proper, which was all that should be granted to attend him.

As soon as he left us, Sir William very politely stepped up to his new niece with a smile, and wished her joy. His example was followed by Miss Wilmot and her father. My wife, too, kissed her daughter with much affection; as, to use her own expression, she was now made an honest woman of. Sophia and Moses followed in turn; and even our benefactor Jenkinson desired to be admitted to that honour. Our satisfaction seemed scarcely capable of increase. Sir William, whose greatest pleasure was in doing good, now looked round with a countenance open as the sun, and saw nothing but joy in the looks of all except that of my daughter Sophia, who, for some reasons we could not comprehend, did not seem perfectly satisfied. "I think now," cried he, with a smile, "that all the company except one or two seem perfectly happy. There only remains an act of justice for me to do. You are sensible, Sir," continued he, turning to me, "of the obligations we both owe to Mr Jenkinson; and it is but just we should both reward him for it. Miss Sophia will, I am sure, make him very happy, and he shall have from me five hundred pounds as her fortune; and upon this I am sure they can live very comfortably together. Come, Miss Sophia, what say you to this match of my making? Will you have him?" My poor girl seemed almost sinking into her mother's arms at the hideous proposal. "Have him, Sir!" cried she faintly; "no, Sir, never!"—"What!" cried he again, "not have Mr Jenkinson, your benefactor, a handsome young fellow, with five hundred pounds, and good expectations?"—"I beg, Sir," returned she, scarce able to speak, "that you'll desist, and not make me so very wretched."—"Was ever such obstinacy known?" cried he again; "to refuse a man whom the family have such infinite obligations to, who has preserved your sister, and who has five hundred pounds! What!

A KISS FROM Mr BURCHELL

not have him!"—"No, Sir, never!" replied she angrily; "I'd sooner die first."—"If that be the case, then," cried he, "if you will not have him—I think I must have you myself." And, so saying, he caught her to his breast with ardour. "My loveliest, my most sensible of girls," cried he, "how could you ever think your own Burchell could deceive you, or that Sir William Thornhill could ever cease to admire a mistress that loved him for himself alone? I have for some years sought for a woman, who, a stranger to my fortune, could think that I had merit as a man. After having tried in vain, even amongst the pert and ugly, how great at last must be my rapture, to have made a conquest over such sense and such heavenly beauty." Then turning to Jenkinson: "As I cannot, Sir, part with this young lady myself, for she has taken a fancy to the cut of my face, all the recompense I can make is to give you her fortune; and you may call upon my steward to-morrow for five hundred pounds." Thus we had all our compliments to repeat, and Lady Thornhill underwent the same round of ceremony that her sister had done before. In the meantime Sir William's gentleman appeared to tell us that the equipages were ready to carry us to the inn, where everything was prepared for our reception. My wife and I led the van, and left those gloomy mansions of sorrow. The generous Baronet ordered forty pounds to be distributed among the prisoners, and Mr Wilmot, induced by his example, gave half that sum. We were received below by the shouts of the villagers, and I saw and shook by the hand two or three of my honest parishioners, who were among the number. They attended us to our inn, where a sumptuous entertainment was provided, and coarser provisions were distributed in great quantities among the populace.

After supper, as my spirits were exhausted by the alternation of pleasure and pain which they had sustained during the day,

I asked permission to withdraw; and, leaving the company in the midst of their mirth, as soon as I found myself alone, I poured out my heart in gratitude to the Giver of joy as well as of sorrow, and then slept undisturbed till morning.

CHAPTER XXXII

THE next morning, as soon as I awaked, I found my eldest son sitting by my bedside, who came to increase my joy with another turn of fortune in my favour. First having released me from the settlement that I had made the day before in his favour, he let me know that my merchant, who had failed in town, was arrested at Antwerp, and there had given up effects to a much greater amount than what was due to his creditors. My boy's generosity pleased me almost as much as this unlooked-for good fortune; but I had some doubts whether I ought, in justice, to accept his offer. While I was pondering upon this Sir William entered the room, to whom I communicated my doubts. His opinion was that, as my son was already possessed of a very affluent fortune by his marriage, I might accept his offer without any hesitation. His business, however, was to inform me, that as he had the night before sent for the licenses, and expected them every hour, he hoped that I would not refuse my assistance in making all the company happy that morning. A footman entered while we were speaking, to tell us that the

207

messenger was returned; and as I was by this time ready, I went down, where I found the whole company as merry as affluence and innocence could make them. However, as they were now preparing for a very solemn ceremony, their laughter entirely displeased me. I told them of the grave, becoming, and sublime deportment they should assume upon this mystical occasion, and read them two homilies, and a thesis of my own composing, in order to prepare them. Yet they still seemed perfectly refractory and ungovernable. Even as we were going along to church, to which I led the way, all gravity had quite forsaken them, and I was often tempted to turn back in indignation. In church a new dilemma arose, which promised no easy solution. This was, which couple should be married first: my son's bride warmly insisted that Lady Thornhill (that was to be) should take the lead; but this the other refused with equal ardour, protesting she would not be guilty of such rudeness for the world. The argument was supported for some time between both, with equal obstinacy and good breeding. But, as I stood all this time with my book ready, I was at last quite tired of the contest; and, shutting it, "I perceive," cried I, "that none of you have a mind to be married, and I think we had as good go back again; for I suppose there will be no business done here to-day." This at once reduced them to reason. The Baronet and his lady were first married, and then my son and his lovely partner.

I had previously, that morning, given orders that a coach should be sent for my honest neighbour Flamborough and his family; by which means, upon our return to the inn, we had the pleasure of finding the two Miss Flamboroughs alighted before us. Mr Jenkinson gave his hand to the eldest, and my son Moses led up the other (and I have since found, that he has taken a real liking to the girl, and my consent and bounty he shall have whenever he thinks proper to demand them). We were no sooner returned to the inn, but numbers of my parishioners, hearing of my success, came to congratulate me; but, amongst the rest, were those who rose to rescue me, and whom I formerly rebuked with such sharpness. I told the story to Sir William, my son-in-law, who went out and reproved them with great sever-ity; but finding them quite disheartened by his harsh reproof he gave them half-a-guinea apiece to drink his health, and raise their dejected spirits.

Soon after this we were called to a very genteel entertain-ment, which was dressed by Mr Thornhill's cook.—And it may not be improper to observe with respect to that gentleman, that he now resides, in quality of companion, at a relation's house, being very well liked, and seldom sitting at the side-table, ex-cept when there is no room at the other; for they make no stranger of him. His time is pretty much taken up in keeping his relation, who is a little melancholy, in spirits, and in learn-ing to blow the French horn. My eldest daughter, however, still remembers him with regret: and she has even told me, though I make a great secret of it, that when he reforms, she may be brought to relent.—But to return, for I am not apt to digress thus; when we were to sit down to dinner, our cere-monies were going to be renewed. The question was, whether my eldest daughter, as being a matron, should not sit above the two young brides; but the debate was cut short by my son George, who proposed that the company should sit indiscrimi-nately, every gentleman by his lady. This was received with great approbation by all, excepting my wife, who, I could per-ceive, was not perfectly satisfied, as she expected to have had the pleasure of sitting at the head of the table, and carving all the meat for all the company. But notwithstanding this, it is im-possible to describe our good humour. I can't say whether we had more wit among us now than usual; but I am certain we had more laughing, which answered the end as well. One jest I particularly remember: old Mr Wilmot drinking to Moses, whose head was turned another way, my son replied, "Madam, I thank you." Upon which the old gentleman, winking upon the rest of the company, observed that he was thinking of his mistress. At which jest I thought the two Miss Flamboroughs would have died with laughing. As soon as dinner was over, according to my old custom, I requested that the table might be taken away to have the pleasure of seeing all my family assembled once more by a cheerful fireside. My two little ones sat upon each knee, the rest of the company by their partners. I had nothing now on this side of the grave to wish for: all my cares were over; my pleasure was unspeakable. It now only remained, that my gratitude in good fortune should exceed my former submission in adversity.

THE ILLUSTRATIONS BY JOHN AUSTEN WERE MADE IN PEN AND IN WATER-COLOR ESPECIALLY FOR THIS EDITION OF "THE VICAR OF WAKEFIELD". THE TYPE USED IS CALEDONIA AND IT IS PRINTED ON A RAG PAPER ESPECIALLY MADE BY THE CURTIS PAPER COMPANY. THE VOLUME WAS DESIGNED BY JOHN S. FASS, AND PRINTED UNDER THE SUPERVISION OF RALPH M. DUENEWALD.